"Don't cry. Please don't cry, Drea," said Derek softly. I could hear his own voice getting hoarse. "We can work it out. You'll see."

"You don't see," I said through the sobs. "It's not going to work. It's gone beyond that. I—I don't think we should date each other anymore."

"Don't say that, Drea," Derek pleaded. "You don't mean it."

I shook my head. "I do. I wish I didn't, but I do."

"No, Drea, I don't believe it. It's a joke, right?"

My only response was silence.

Bantam Sweet Dreams Romances
Ask your bookseller for the books you have missed

1 P.S. I LOVE YOU
2 THE POPULARITY PLAN
3 LAURIE'S SONG
4 PRINCESS AMY
5 LITTLE SISTER
6 CALIFORNIA GIRL
7 GREEN EYES
8 THE THOROUGHBRED
9 COVER GIRL
10 LOVE MATCH
11 THE PROBLEM WITH LOVE
12 NIGHT OF THE PROM
13 THE SUMMER JENNY FELL IN LOVE
14 DANCE OF LOVE
16 HOW DO YOU SAY GOODBYE?
17 ASK ANNIE
18 TEN BOY SUMMER
19 LOVE SONG
20 THE POPULARITY SUMMER
22 SECRET IDENTITY
23 FALLING IN LOVE AGAIN
24 THE TROUBLE WITH CHARLIE
26 IT MUST BE MAGIC
29 NEVER LOVE A COWBOY
30 LITTLE WHITE LIES
32 DAYDREAMER
35 FORBIDDEN LOVE
36 SUMMER DREAMS
39 FIRST LOVE
41 THE TRUTH ABOUT ME AND BOBBY V
45 DREAM PROM
47 TE AMO MEANS I LOVE YOU
48 DIAL L FOR LOVE
49 TOO MUCH TO LOSE
50 LIGHTS, CAMERA, LOVE
53 GHOST OF A CHANCE
54 I CAN'T FORGET YOU
55 SPOTLIGHT ON LOVE
56 CAMPFIRE NIGHTS
57 ON HER OWN
58 RHYTHM OF LOVE
59 PLEASE SAY YES
60 SUMMER BREEZES
61 EXCHANGE OF HEARTS
62 JUST LIKE THE MOVIES
63 KISS ME, CREEP
64 LOVE IN THE FAST LANE
65 THE TWO OF US
66 LOVE TIMES TWO
67 I BELIEVE IN YOU
68 LOVEBIRDS
69 CALL ME BEAUTIFUL
70 SPECIAL SOMEONE
71 TOO MANY BOYS
72 GOODBYE FOREVER
73 LANGUAGE OF LOVE
74 DON'T FORGET ME
75 FIRST SUMMER LOVE
76 THREE CHEERS FOR LOVE
77 TEN-SPEED SUMMER
78 NEVER SAY NO
79 STAR STRUCK
80 A SHOT AT LOVE
81 SECRET ADMIRER
82 HEY, GOOD LOOKING!
83 LOVE BY THE BOOK
84 THE LAST WORD
85 THE BOY SHE LEFT BEHIND
86 QUESTIONS OF LOVE
87 PROGRAMMED FOR LOVE
88 WRONG KIND OF BOY
89 101 WAYS TO MEET MR. RIGHT
90 TWO'S A CROWD
91 THE LOVE HUNT
92 KISS AND TELL
93 THE GREAT BOY CHASE
94 SECOND CHANCES

Too Close for Comfort

Debra Spector

BANTAM BOOKS
TORONTO • NEW YORK • LONDON • SYDNEY

RL 6, IL age 11 and up

TOO CLOSE FOR COMFORT
A Bantam Book / February 1983
Reprinted 1983
Reprinted 1985

Cover photo by Pat Hill

ISBN 0-553-17839-3

Published simultaneously in the United States and Canada

Bantam Books are published by Bantam Books, Inc. Its trademark, consisting of the words "Bantam Books" and the portrayal of a rooster, is registered in U.S. Patent and Trademark Office and in other countries. Marca Registrada. Bantam Books, Inc., 666 Fifth Avenue, New York, New York 10103.

Printed and bound in Great Britain by Hunt Barnard Printing Ltd.

O 0 9 8 7 6 5 4 3 2 1

Too Close for Comfort

Chapter One

"Ooh," I said, rushing through the back door of my house and slamming my books down on the kitchen counter.

"Andrea's in a rotten mood," my sister Natalie cooed, looking up from the table where she was doing her homework.

"It's Drea," I told her pointedly. "How many times do I have to tell you, that's what I want to be called now!" Angrily I took off my Seminole Grove cheerleader's jacket and flung it over the back of one of the wooden chairs.

"I think it's stupid," Natalie declared, turning her attention back to her notebook full of math problems.

"It's not stupid," I said, not quite ready to end the discussion. "It's different, that's all—and I happen to like it."

"Suit yourself." She shrugged and looked up again. "But what's that got to do with what you're all steamed up about?" She paused a minute before adding, "Trouble with Roger, huh?"

"You wouldn't understand," I said uncomfortably, reaching into the refrigerator for some eggs and butter. "You're too young."

"I knew it. It *is* Roger," she concluded. "And what makes you think I wouldn't understand? I'm twelve, you know."

Natalie really looked insulted; she shot a look at me like I was a dummy or something. It made me feel a little guilty for tearing into her—after all, I wasn't mad at her, she just happened to be a convenient target.

"Look, I'm sorry," I began, taking a bowl out of one of the kitchen cabinets. "Roger broke up with me today, and I'm just so upset I—"

"You're going to make brownies, aren't you?" she asked.

My dear, devoted, and observant sister Natalie. She knew that whenever I got upset about something I'd cheer myself up by baking a batch of brownies. It was a silly habit, I suppose, especially since I always cursed myself afterward for eating them. But there was just something so warm and comforting about the smell of freshly made brownies. And if there ever was a day I needed to feel warm and comforted. . . .

I turned to face my little sister. "I'll make you a deal. You can have some, if you pick up your stuff and do your homework somewhere else. I feel like being alone for a while, OK?"

That was all the incentive Natalie needed. "Sure thing," she said, picking up her books as soon as the words were out of my mouth. "I was about to stop anyway. It's almost time for *General Hospital.* I'll be in our room if you need me. Ta-ta." At the doorway she turned around and almost as an afterthought said, "Oh, sorry about Roger. But I never liked him anyway."

"Thanks, Nat." I sighed. "I needed that."

As Natalie went off to commiserate with her soap opera heroines over their lost loves, I returned to thoughts of my own lost love. While I mixed up the brownie batter, my mind kept replaying that scene by my locker after school. The whole thing couldn't have lasted more than a minute—although the shock gave it long-lasting effects.

It had been a pretty good day up till then, too. Mr. Billings, my marine biology teacher, had complimented me on my report on dolphin intelligence. That meant a lot to me; in the past year I'd developed an interest in the sea, especially in the marine life right here off the Florida coast. Then, at cheerleading practice right after school, I finally got all the way through the new cheer for Friday night's homecoming game, without even missing a beat. That meant a lot to me, too—the last thing in the world I wanted to do was mess up at homecoming, which at our school was the biggest game of the year.

I was still a little heady from the practice when I went back to my locker and found Roger, my boyfriend of nearly two months, pacing up and down the dingy yellow hall. It looked as if he had been waiting for me there since school let out. I don't know if the wait did it, but he didn't waste time once I got there. Not even giving me a chance to say hi, he matter-of-factly announced he didn't want to see me anymore, that we were through. Just like that. No warning, no second chance. Boy, he had some nerve, I thought, as I stood there in shock. Right before the homecoming dance, too!

The situation was just too depressing for words. As I sat waiting for the brownies to bake, I rested my head on the table and moped. A little self-pity never hurt anybody, I thought, and I did have a lot to feel sorry about. I had thought Roger really liked me.

"Hey, Drea, what's the matter?"

The screen door to the kitchen slammed shut with a bang. Raising my head, I turned to face my next-door neighbor and good friend Derek. His smiling face was a stark contrast to my now tear-streaked one. "Derek, I'm depressed," I blurted out.

"I can tell," he said, taking a whiff of the aroma that filled the room. "Brownies again." Derek's sunny, dimpled expression was infectious, and I felt my spirits rise a little. "It's Rog, isn't it?" he asked.

"How did you know?"

"There's only one thing that would drive you to brownies this close to a big dance—boy trouble."

Shaking my head at his insight and the way he always tuned into my boy problems, I said in a rush, "He dumped me, Derek. Just like that. What am I going to do?"

Derek pulled out a chair, turned it around, and sat down, resting his arms on the top of it. "Seems like you need the services of Derek Sebastian, adviser to the lovelorn."

I smiled, wiping away one last tear from my red-rimmed eyes. "You always have an answer for everything, don't you?"

"Only for you, it seems," he said affectionately, reaching over to muss up my hair. "Maybe this'll help. I've got some news that might cheer you up. Interested?"

I dropped my self-pity long enough to see that Derek was still beaming, as if he had something to say that could hardly wait. Of course he did, dummy, I told myself. Why else would he have burst in here like he did? "Sure, Derek," I said. "What's up?"

"You're looking at the Indians' new starting receiver," he said proudly. "Coach has given me the nod for the homecoming game!"

"That's sensational!" I screamed. This was

Derek's first year on the varsity football team. Getting this chance to play against West Fort Lauderdale High, our biggest rival, was making him glow with self-confidence, and here I was, spoiling his good news. Slapping him five, I added, beaming, "I'm so proud of you!"

"See, I've cheered you up already." He grinned in a way I always found kind of cute.

"No, I mean it. Coach Jenkins must think you're something pretty special."

Derek reddened a little, his little-boy shyness mixing with his newly found pride. "Well, he did like the way I caught those passes in the Port Everglades game. Said he likes the way I've developed."

"I'd say that's an understatement," I said, although I didn't mean it the way the coach did. Over the summer Derek had grown in every which way, from a skinny little kid to a . . . well, to a tall and attractive young man. He was a little over six feet tall now, and the brassy bright hair that had earned him the hated nickname "Red" when he was a kid had darkened to a mahoganylike shade that any girl would kill for. His slightly round face and fading freckles still gave him a boyish appearance, but that, too, was beginning to change.

Just then the oven buzzer went off, and I got up to retrieve the brownies, setting the pan on a hot plate on the table. But as soon as I put them down, Derek got up, took a knife out of the drawer, picked up a potholder, and grabbed the pan.

"What are you doing, Derek?" I asked.

"I'm nuts for your brownies," he said, picking up the hot plate in his other hand and heading toward the doorway that led to the rest of the house.

"They're still hot. You'll get a stomachache."

"I'll chance it," he said. "Bring the milk and join me in the family room."

Obligingly I grabbed the milk and a couple of glasses and followed him to the family room, where I found him seated in my father's leather easy chair, the brownies on the table beside him. I took a seat on the couch—aware of what he was up to now. Derek the counselor was open for business, as he usually was when it concerned my trouble with boys.

"I'm ready whenever you are," I said.

"So what happend with Roger?" he wanted to know.

I rested my head against one of my mother's needlepoint pillows and told him very simply what had happened—that Roger had wasted no words in telling me that he had no interest in seeing me anymore.

"The guy must have no brains," Derek said, reaching to cut a brownie. "Ouch, it's hot!"

"Told you," I said, rolling my eyes good-naturedly at him. Then, feeling that my situation was hopeless, I let out a sigh. "Derek, what am I going to do—the homecoming dance is Saturday!"

Derek sat back, cupping his hands around his right knee, thinking. "Something's puzzling me, Drea. Are you upset because Roger's gone or because you don't have a date for the dance?"

"What do you mean?" I asked.

Derek poured himself another glass of milk and cut another brownie. "Mmm, these are delish. Have one."

"Why, thank you," I said with mock indignation as he cut one for me. They were *my* brownies, after all.

Derek wiped away the crumbs from his mouth. "How much did you like Roger?"

"He was nice—" I began.

"Nice," Derek mused, letting the word hang in the air. "Nice is always a nice word to use when you really mean something else. Seems to me I remember you complaining last week about how Roger's favorite topic of conversation was Roger."

"That's true."

"And that he hates what you did with your hair."

"Yeah," I agreed, reaching for another brownie. Last month, tired of having to fuss with it, I got my shoulder-length, light-brown hair cut real short. I thought it made me look better—and I liked how much easier it was to take care of. But Roger hated it. He thought it made me look boyish, and to prove it he even began calling me Andrew. "That must have been the beginning of the end," I reflected aloud, realizing that no boy could stay interested in a girl he called Andrew for very long.

"Well, I think it looks cute on you."

"What does?"

"Your hair. Now I can see your face."

"Thanks. That's nice of you to say—even if you do sound like my mother."

"Well, I mean it." Derek lowered his hazel eyes, as if he were embarrassed a little by his admission. Though he had matured in his appearance and become more outgoing, Derek still found it hard to talk to girls, let alone compliment them. I was about the only girl I knew with whom he felt comfortable, but then he'd known me for so long I think he sometimes felt responsible for me, like he was my big brother or something. Sometimes, though, Derek was so protective of me that he almost seemed jealous if a boy paid me the least bit of attention.

"OK, so I'll admit Roger *wasn't* the love of my life. Then why do I feel so miserable?"

"Simple. You're upset because you don't have a date for the dance. Admit it, that's what's really eating you."

I let my third brownie melt in my mouth before I answered. "I suppose you're right."

"I knew it," he said, putting down his empty glass.

"OK, smart guy, what am I going to do? The dance is only four days away!"

Derek poured the last few remaining drops from the milk carton into his glass. "I can't think on an empty stomach," he said, rising. "I'm going to get more milk. Want some?"

"Sure," I said as I watched him head toward the kitchen.

Derek really was special, I thought as I waited for him to return. He always seemed to be around whenever something had happened in my life—and not just when I had problems with boys but also when I had fights with my parents, disappointments at school, or whatever. And here he was again. It was as if he had a sixth sense that told him I needed someone to talk to, someone to whom I could vent my feelings and who would know enough to keep the contents of the conversation to himself.

Derek came back with the milk and filled up both glasses. "All I could find was this no-fat stuff."

"Don't sound so glum. It's good for the figure," I said, pointing to my hips. Although I'm not fat, it's a never-ending struggle to stay that way. And eating half a pan of brownies certainly doesn't help.

"There's nothing wrong with them," Derek said before gulping down his milk. He grimaced. "This stuff is too watery."

"Sorry," I replied. "I'll have to tell Mom to put in a supply of regular milk just for you."

"Thanks," he said. Derek sat back and in a quiet voice added, "I think I may have a solution to your problem, Drea."

"Oh, yeah?" I challenged. "Well, speak up, O Wise One."

"While I was in the kitchen I—um—thought of someone who's looking for a date."

"You did?" Derek always seemed to come up with a solution to my problems, but I never expected him to come up with another boy on such short notice. "Who?" I said excitedly, all thoughts of Roger rapidly retreating into my memory banks. "Someone I know?"

"Yeah," he answered slowly.

"Is he on the team?"

Derek nodded.

"Is he tall?" I asked, knowing that Derek knew I was partial to tall guys.

"Uh-huh."

"Nice?"

"You could say that."

I was dying of curiosity, but this guessing game of Derek's was trying my patience. "OK," I said, knowing this would be the last question I would have to ask. "Who is it?"

The smiling, dimpled expression on Derek's face turned serious. "Me. Would you like to go with me, Drea?"

"You mean it, don't you?" I breathed with nervous excitement.

Derek leaned forward and nodded his head, his eyebrows arched slightly in hopeful anticipation. "Do you want to?"

"Are you kidding? I'd love to!" I answered quickly, my heart racing wildly as the thought danced in my head: *Derek, what took you so long?*

Chapter Two

"Oh, where is he?" I wondered out loud in nervous anticipation. It was Friday night, just minutes away from the kickoff of the homecoming game, and I was in my customary spot in front of the stands, which were filled with Seminole Grove boosters.

"Hey, lighten up." My friend Jane, overhearing me, came over and gave me a reassuring pat on the shoulder. "The team's not due for several minutes yet."

"I can't help it. I'm just so nervous for him," I said, still focusing my eyes on the narrow dirt path linking the field to the Indians' locker room.

Jane's hearty laugh made me turn around. "What's so funny?" I asked.

"You," she answered. "I've never seen you so hyper."

"Well, Derek's never started a game before."

Jane shook her head. "I guess I shouldn't be

so hard on you. I remember getting pretty antsy myself the first time Randy played. Still it's kind of funny to see your reaction—you two haven't even gone out yet."

"That's only because he had late practice all week. Anyway, I feel like his girlfriend, and I want to keep an eye out for him."

"I don't know how you'll see him with all those stars in front of your eyes," Jane said and winked.

I hoped my concern for Derek didn't make me blow the new cheer we were going to do that night for the first time. It was the brainstorm of Kathy Lewis, the co-captain of the squad. She felt that since we were the Seminole Grove Indians, we should have at least one cheer in the Seminole language. Kathy really did her homework on this, managing to get the words from an elderly chief at the nearby Seminole reservation. The cheer itself was simple—"Go Indians. You're the best. Go Indians. Better than the rest"—but saying it in Seminole was a big challenge. It was bad enough having to worry about Derek on the field; having to cope with a new language and be enthusiastic about it at the same time was driving me crazy.

The sound of the band marching onto the field for the opening ceremonies jolted me back to attention. I joined Jane, Kathy, and the rest of the squad in a quick warm-up cheer. Then, at the sounds of static from the public address system, we all leaned closer to the fence, preparing to wave our pom-poms at the first glimpse of the team.

Our rivals, the West Fort Lauderdale Sun Devils, were the first team to be announced—and even from my vantage point across the field, they looked awesome.

Then, with our band leading a fanfare, our team took the field. The crowd didn't even need cheerleaders—a big roar went up when Clark Whitfield was announced. A senior, he was the team's latest hero, having run for two touchdowns in the final two minutes of last week's game, leading the team to a come-from-behind victory.

And then came Derek. The big lump that had been sitting in my heart all evening rose to my throat—and I was glad I didn't have to do any complicated routines right then. Another roar rose from the crowd, not as big as the one for Clark, but then this was Derek's first varsity homecoming game. Derek had a huge smile plastered on his face as he ran to his position on the bench. A second later he turned around and caught my eye, and I threw a little kiss in his direction.

After the band played the "Star-spangled Banner," Clark walked to midfield to join the Sun Devils' captain for the coin toss. The other team won and got the ball first, and I stood up and led the crowd in one of our defense cheers.

Out team looked like they were trying their hardest, but the Sun Devils had too much going for them and scored an easy touchdown.

Then it was our turn. The first two plays were runs, and neither one netted much yardage. It was obvious the next play would be a pass, and I bit my lip nervously. Just let Derek catch the ball, I prayed silently over and over until the ball was snapped. It was a pass all right—but to the other receiver, a senior named Hank, who dropped it. I then turned my gaze to Derek, and I knew from the way he carried himself back to the bench that he, like the rest of us, was very disappointed.

"Derek'll get it the next time around," Jane said optimistically as our team punted the ball back to the Sun Devils.

Unfortunately, her football analysis was way off. The entire first half belonged to our rivals. Although they were able to score only one other touchdown, they dominated the play and didn't give our team much time with the ball. Derek still hadn't had the opportunity to catch anything, and I knew he must have felt really frustrated.

At halftime I left Jane and joined the rest of the crowd at the refreshment stands. Although our team hadn't yet scored, I'd put in an active first half joining the other cheerleaders in pepping up the crowd's enthusiasm. My throat was raw from all that yelling, and I needed a drink.

"Hey, Drea. Andrea Mallory," I heard someone call softly just then. Turning around, however, I didn't see anyone I knew.

"Drea, over here."

Stepping on my tiptoes, I saw the small hand of Mary Jo McKenzie, a girl I knew from PE class. She was ahead of me in line and was waving to me to join her.

Mary Jo couldn't have been more than five feet tall, and it was a little difficult getting to her in the crowd. But she didn't waste any time getting to the point. "I wanted to let you know I'm so sorry about what happened," she told me, shaking her head solemnly.

"What happened?" I didn't have the slightest idea what she was talking about.

Now she was the puzzled one. "I mean you and Roger," she explained.

"Oh, that," I scoffed lightly. "Not to worry. We weren't meant to last, that's all."

"Terrific," she said, smiling broadly, showing off her perfectly straight teeth. "Oops, I mean, I'm glad you feel that way. You see, Roger's taking me to the dance tomorrow, and I'd feel *just awful* if I thought I was doing anything to hurt you."

"Forget it," I told her gallantly. I found her false sweetness irritating, but I knew better than to tell her to her face what I truly felt about Roger—she would spread the news to the whole junior class by the end of the third quarter. "I hope you have better luck with him than I did. Besides, I'll be there with Derek Sebastian."

She smiled with relief. "I'm glad to hear that." We were at the head of the line now and gave our orders to the frazzled counterman. While we waited, Mary Jo said, "You must really be grateful you have a friend like Derek to fall back on."

"Hey, he's not doing me any favors," I said, a little upset with her insinuation. "We're going to the dance together because we want to, not because we have to."

"Sorry," she purred. "I just thought since you two were friends—"

I shook my head. "Huh-uh. In fact, I think Roger may have actually done me a favor," I said. "Derek was just waiting for the opportunity to ask me out but didn't want to as long as Roger was in the picture." I didn't know this for a fact, but it sounded reasonable enough.

I paid for my drink and moved out of the line. "Well, thanks for letting me cut in," I said. "I appreciate it."

"See you at the dance, maybe," Mary Jo said. "And thanks for being such a dear about Roger."

No problem, I thought. You two deserve each other.

A few minutes later, I was back in front of the stands, waiting for the second half to begin. Our band was just winding up their routine, so I knew it wouldn't be long to kickoff.

But when the team took the field to begin play, Derek was not among them. I spotted his number, eighty-four, on the far corner of the bench. "Why is the coach benching him?" I wondered aloud to Jane.

"Beats me," she said. "It's not his fault he didn't catch anything in the first half. Maybe the coach just wants to use Hank instead."

"It's not fair," I replied as I eyed Derek sitting slumped over on the bench, the smile he wore during the first half replaced by a serious frown. Being given the position as the Indians' new starting receiver was a big boon to Derek, whose self-confidence was often on the shaky side. Ever since I'd known Derek, it seemed that it was easier for him to cheer up his friends than it was for him to cheer up himself.

Seeing him there reminded me how Derek and I first became friends in the true sense of the word. It happened the spring we were both going on eight. My dad was coaching a local Little League team, and I begged him to let me be on it, even though my skills with a bat were slightly better than disastrous. Derek was on the team, too, only he was forced on it by his mom, who felt it would help him take his mind off *it*—his parents' divorce of the previous winter. Derek wasn't much of a ballplayer in those days (you should see him now, though!), so he ended up spending a lot of time with me on the bench.

My heart went out to Derek that spring. We'd talk about the game, or about some dumb TV show, or just sit there without talking at all. Soon I began to look forward to the games more for Derek's company than for my all-too-rare appearances at the plate. Slowly I could tell Derek was beginning to feel the same way about me, and by the time the Little League championship had been decided, we'd both made a pact vowing to be each other's best friend forever.

"I wish I could run over to Derek and tell him he didn't do anything wrong," I said to Jane midway through the third quarter.

"I think he knows that," she said. "Tonight is just not the Indians' night. Nobody's playing well." By now it had become apparent that our team was destined to lose, and the cheering had become harder and harder to do.

By the time the fourth quarter rolled around, the coach must have had a change of heart, for he put Derek back in the game. On the first play in, Derek caught a pass for a first down, and the crowd perked up. I was sure my shouts could be heard above the rest, even more so on the next play, when once again Derek caught a pass, this time for a twenty-five-yard gain. At last the team was on the move, and something was working right. Several running plays gained more yardage, and before I knew it, the team was down near the goal line.

I could hardly contain myself then. I was only

glad I could vent my nervousness through my cheering with the others. We were so close, we just had to score! I closed my eyes for a second, almost afraid to see what was going to happen next. In that moment the center snapped the ball to Clark, who fired a quick pass to Derek in the end zone. Touchdown!

Derek must have jumped ten feet in the air. I didn't see what happened next on the field since I was too busy hugging Jane and the rest of the squad, all of us near tears. Up went purple and white streamers in the stands; the place looked like it was ready to explode.

I wish I could say that the team went on to score two more touchdowns in the final minutes to put the game in our hands, but nothing of the sort happened. Soon afterward, the Sun Devils came back to score again and put the game out of reach. Final score: Sun Devils 21–Indians 7.

But Derek got to be a hero—if only for a moment. And if the coach didn't have his silly rule against partying right after the game, I would have shown Derek my appreciation right then and there. As it was, I'd just have to wait for the dance.

Chapter Three

I would have preferred to have spent all day Saturday getting ready for the dance, making sure every single detail was put to rest, but Mom had other ideas for me. She made me take Natalie to the Broward mall that afternoon to get her new shoes. Mom didn't trust Natalie to go off with her friends—the last time Mom did, Natalie came back with a pair of green and orange shoes that never made an appearance out of her closet.

As soon as I walked into the shoe store, I picked up a plain but adequate pair of flats and handed them to her. "Here, take these."

"Yecch," she said, quickly dropping them back on the rack. "They have holes in them."

"They're supposed to. It's a design," I said.

"Well, I like these," she said, pointing to a pair of penny loafers.

"Since when have you gone preppy?"

"Wendy got a pair like these last week," she told me.

"Fine," I said. "Let's take them. I've got to get home, I don't have much time to get ready."

Natalie looked at her watch. "What are you talking about? It's only one o'clock."

"Is that all?"

"Yeah, and Mom said we could eat here. I'm hungry."

I shrugged. "OK." After paying for the shoes, I followed Natalie to the part of the mall where all the fast-food restaurants were located. As usual, the place was packed with kids from all over the area—this was a favorite people-watching place, and I could feel plenty of eyes looking me over as we waited on line at the health-food stand.

We couldn't find an empty table, so we had to eat leaning against a railing. Natalie didn't seem to mind, though—in fact, she was enjoying the opportunity to survey the territory. She'd reached the point where she was beginning to discover boys but hadn't had the nerve to do anything about it.

"See anything you like?" I asked.

Natalie feigned ignorance. "What are you talking about?"

"It's OK, Nat," I said. "I know Mom didn't say anything about lunch. You just wanted to go boy-watching, right?"

She blushed. "How did you know?"

"I recognize that look in your eye," I said, putting down my fork. "Looks like you found a winner."

Natalie smiled impishly, her emerald-green eyes shining, and brushed a stray strand of her long brown hair behind her ear. "That one over there," she said, indicating a group of boys in their early teens near the baked-potato stand. "The one with the blue jacket. He's kind of cute."

The boy had a roundish, freckled face and bright red hair. He looked remarkably like Derek did a few years ago. "Hmm, I didn't know you were partial to redheads."

"Why not? After all, I'm the one who's responsible for putting you and Derek together."

"Oh, really? How do you figure that?"

Natalie took a spoonful of her frozen yogurt, then said, "Remember the first time you two took me trick-or-treating on Halloween?"

"Sure," I said. Derek and I were eight, and our moms thought it'd be cute if we escorted four-year-old Natalie around the neighborhood. "How can you remember back that far?"

"I don't really. But Mom reminded me the other day how I went around to all the houses, telling everyone you were my 'mommy and daddy.' I had you two pegged way back then."

"As I recall, we didn't think much of the idea at the time."

"Maybe. But I knew that sooner or later you'd

get together. Personally, I think you'd be a fool not to. I think his red hair is sexy."

"I guess I've always liked him, but his hair is the least of it." I took a sip of my orange drink and watched as Natalie returned her attention to the scenery. "Who now?" I asked.

"That guy over there with the rugby shirt," she said, pointing to the pizza counter. "He's pretty terrific-looking, too."

"Just remember one thing: looks aren't everything," I pointed out wisely. "The boys with the drop-dead looks usually turn out to be real jerks—like Roger."

"Derek's good-looking."

"He's nice-looking, sure, but I wouldn't call him gorgeous," I said. "But I'd like him even if he were ugly. I've always felt relaxed and comfortable around him."

"It's better that way, isn't it?"

"I think so," I answered.

"I wish Mom and Dad would let me go out," Natalie said, licking the edges of her spoon.

"They let you go to school dances and stuff."

"It's not the same. I'd like a real boyfriend like Derek."

"Your time will come," I assured her, pausing to look at my watch. "You finished?"

"It's only a quarter to two, Drea."

"And I've got a long afternoon ahead of me. Let's go. You can help me get ready for the dance."

I spent the rest of that afternoon in my room, talking to Natalie in between countless calls back and forth with Jane, ironing my knickers four times to get out *all* the wrinkles, and showering twice. I didn't feel I needed to impress Derek, but I did want to look nice for our first real date together. I finally put on my olive-green knickers and the gold and green sweater that went with it. It hit the perfect middle note, not too casual and not too dressy either.

At exactly seven-thirty Derek rang the doorbell, and I ran to answer it. "Well, hello there," I said sweetly, then gasped when I saw what he was wearing.

He grinned and said, "They're going to call us the Bobbsey twins or something." He was wearing olive-green cords and a green-striped shirt.

I smelled something funny in the air. Taking a deep whiff, I twitched my nose in displeasure.

Derek noticed and mumbled. "It's my after-shave. I guess I put too much on, huh?"

"But you don't shave," I noted. Derek's skin was still smooth, without a trace of the stubble I sometimes saw on other boys.

"I wanted to smell nice for you," he said apologetically.

I felt like a crumb, forgetting how sensitive Derek could be about himself. "You didn't have to do that," I said, "but it was real sweet of you."

Mom and Dad came into the hallway then,

anxious to see us off. "Why, don't you look nice, Derek," Mom said.

"Thanks, Mrs. Mallory," he replied politely.

I could see Mom sniffing the air, but thankfully she didn't say another word. I think Derek was embarrassed enough as it was.

"Have a good time, you two," Dad said. "But not too good—if you know what I mean."

"Daddy," I groaned, shaking my head. "I think we'd better be going," I said to Derek.

"Don't worry, Mr. Mallory," Derek added. "I'll take good care of your daughter, won't do anything to be ashamed of, and won't keep her out too late." To me he whispered, "That's what you're supposed to say to parents, right?"

I winked playfully. "You ready?"

"Anytime you are. You've got the keys."

Because Derek's learner's permit only allowed him to drive during the day, I had to drive to the dance. Not that I minded; I had gotten my license in August, and I jumped at every chance to take out the car. We walked across the lawn to the driveway, where my mother's Chevy was parked.

"Well, that wasn't as bad as I thought it'd be," Derek said after we got into the car. "I was afraid your parents would say lots of stuff about how cute we looked and what a lovely couple we made."

"I think they know better."

"It's a good thing you didn't see my mom.

She was on my case all day telling me what to do and what to say and all that."

"Now why in the world would you need to be told what to say to me?"

Derek looked out the window. "You know," he hedged. "I mean, we've never been out on a date before. Or more accurately, *I've* never been out on a date before."

"So what?" I told him. "Don't you realize we've already overcome the hardest hurdle in dating?"

"We have?"

"Sure. Most guys, when they ask a girl out, really don't know the girl that well. Oh, they may talk a lot in class or about general school stuff, but when it comes to really knowing what the girl is like, they don't know. Same with the girl. Well, Derek, you already know me. All we do on a date is talk about the things we always talk about." I paused. "Well, that's not *all* we do on a date, but you get my drift, don't you?"

"Yeah," he said, reaching for my hand, which I'd conveniently let drop from the steering wheel.

We were both silent for a while, and in no time at all we were at the high school. I had no trouble finding a parking space and gingerly guided the car into a spot between two cars.

Derek looked at me before we got out. "Drea, I want to tell you something before we go inside."

"Go ahead."

"I'm not sure if you know this or not, but I didn't ask you out just because Roger broke up with you. It's something I've wanted to do for a long time."

"I'm glad to hear that," I said, smiling. "Though if I'd known sooner, I'd have gotten rid of Roger a long time ago."

"Let's go in then," he said, abruptly opening his door. We joined the dozens of other couples filing into the gym. The place was already filled. Derek led me through the crowd to the refreshment table at the far corner, where we both stood and checked the place out.

Derek offered me a glass of watery fruit punch. "Here's to us," he said. Looking around, he added awkwardly, "Happy homecoming."

"Happy homecoming," I repeated, touching my paper cup to his. "Looks like most of the gang is here."

"Yeah," he said, downing his drink in one gulp. "Want to dance?"

"I thought you'd never ask," I said.

The student deejay was spinning a slow song, and I was surprised at the smooth way Derek was leading me across the slippery floor. "I didn't know you could dance," I admitted to him afterward.

He arched his eyebrows and grinned. "We have no secrets, right?"

I nodded.

"Promise you won't laugh if I tell you something."

"I promise," I said, still puzzled.

"I made my mom practice with me all week. I didn't want to embarrass you."

"Derek, you didn't have to do that. Besides, you're a natural at it."

"I don't know," he admitted. "Wait until the fast ones. Mom didn't know any of those."

But Derek was just as good on the fast dances. It didn't take him long to master the moves, and he was able to improvise on them so well it got him the attention of those around us.

But I must admit I was partial to the slow dances, when Derek would hold me securely in his arms. We'd be so close I could hear the steady pounding of his heart. Every now and again he would tentatively touch my neck, sending shivers down my back—delightful shivers, that is. That touch would make me nuzzle up just a little closer. It felt so natural I wished Derek had asked me out long before this.

Just about everyone at the dance seemed happy to see us together, too. Derek's teammates really seemed surprised to see him with a girl, period, and all night long they teased him. Some even made suggestive comments I'd rather not repeat, but even they were said with such lightheartedness that I couldn't really be offended.

But as much as I liked being with Derek, I liked being sociable, too. So, at several points along the way when other boys asked me to dance, I accepted their invitations. I encouraged

Derek to dance with other girls, too, especially since he was so new at it and enjoying the experience. I even went so far as to point out a few girls standing alone near the door who looked like they'd love the opportunity. But Derek didn't want to, preferring instead to huddle with his teammates and analyze what went wrong in the game. He'd look at me dancing, though, and every time I looked back, I could see him staring intensely at me. Could he be jealous? I wondered.

About two hours into the dance, we caught up with Jane and Randy at the refreshment table. "I was wondering when you two would take some time out to be with your friends," Jane teased.

"I'm still in training," Derek answered. "I've got to stay in shape. Dancing's great exercise."

"Especially the slow ones, right?" Randy said pointedly.

"What's the matter, Randy?" I put in. "Jealous?"

Derek handed me another cup of punch as Jane pointed to the middle of the dance floor. "I think someone else in this room is jealous. Have you seen the way Roger's been looking at you all night?"

"No," I said, "and I don't particularly care."

"That's right," Derek added, looking a little uncomfortable. "He's her former boyfriend."

A passing dancer accidentally bumped into me just then, knocking the cup of punch all over my sweater and pants. "Oh, no!" I screeched. "What a mess!"

"Let's clean you off," Jane said. Then to the boys she added, "Don't do anything silly while we're gone."

We snaked our way through the crowd to the bathroom down the hall. Finding a sink available, I dabbed at the punch stains, while casting an odd look at my friend. "What was the idea of bringing Roger up in front of Derek?" I asked.

"I thought you'd want to know," Jane answered, taking the time to comb out her straight blond hair.

"Not really," I said. "I haven't thought about him in days. Even if I had, I still think it was weird for you to talk about him in front of Derek."

"Why? Derek knows all about him."

"Let me ask you something. If I was with another boy, would you have said something?"

"Of course not."

"So why treat Derek differently? We're on a date tonight, you know."

Jane sighed and reached into her bag for her lip gloss. "I still have a hard time thinking of you two as boyfriend and girlfriend."

"Well, start trying. I have a feeling this is going to work."

Jane turned to face me. "You're really having a good time with him?"

"Better than I've had with any other date in a long time."

"Well, I hope it works out for you."

"You seem doubtful."

"You two are such good friends. I'd hate to see you lose that."

"Why should we? I think we're only going to become better friends as we go along."

"And what's going to happen when you break up with each other?"

"Who said anything about breaking up? This is only our first date!"

As we left the bathroom, Jane spotted Randy. I found Derek still standing by the punch bowl, talking with Clark about yesterday's game. I don't know if Jane's remarks had anything to do with it, but I was glad Derek wasn't off dancing with another girl—right now I wanted him all to myself. Self-assuredly, I went up to him and linked my arm through his.

Clark finished his sentence and then said to me, "I was telling Derek he'd better be careful now that he's out with a cheerleader. You girls have a reputation for eating us guys alive."

"I think Derek's old enough to take care of himself," I said good-naturedly. "Besides, I know you guys will be watching me to make sure I behave well."

"Now that I have your assurances, I think I'll leave you two alone," Clark said, looking around the room for his date. "See you at practice, Sebastian."

I urged Derek onto the dance floor just as another slow song came up. Only a few lights were on in the gym now, giving the room a dark, mysterious flavor that made me feel romantic. I held Derek close again and whispered into his ear what a wonderful time I was having. He didn't say anything, but he pulled me away for a moment, smiled, and gave me a little kiss on my nose.

"That's sweet, Derek," I breathed. "What do you say we leave now?"

Puzzled, he looked at me for a moment, then shrugged and said, "OK."

Excitedly, I thought ahead to the wonderful moments we would be spending together alone. I pictured us driving out to this secluded spot at the beach Derek and I had discovered as kids. It was just big enough and high enough off the water for two people to sit and watch the ocean lap onto the shore. We used to toss pebbles into the ocean from that elevated point, but for tonight I had something more romantic in mind. The moon was nearly full, and I pictured how beautiful its reflection would look on the water as I cuddled up in Derek's warm arms.

When Derek asked if he could drive back, I didn't hesitate to say yes. I didn't see any harm in it since he'd just finished his driver's ed class and would have his license in a matter of weeks. Maybe he even had a special place of his own that he wanted to show me.

Like a pro he guided the car out of the parking lot and down Seminole Grove's main street. "Where are we going?" I asked at the first red light.

"Home," he answered.

I felt deflated. Didn't he have the same feelings I had? Something kept me from asking him, though, and all I said was, "Oh."

Derek looked at me. "You sound surprised. Where else did you think I'd be taking you? You know I promised your parents I wouldn't keep you out too late."

"I see." Maybe he had been thinking about going someplace else but was deterred by the thought of what my parents would say.

"Drea," he said when the light changed and we got rolling again, "I want you to know I really had a good time with you tonight."

"Me, too, Derek."

"Do you think you might want to do it again sometime?"

"Oh, yes," I said, glad to see that his interest in me at the dance was genuine. "Maybe next time, just the two of us."

"Great," he said. "I was afraid you'd think I wasn't experienced enough for you. It would have really bothered me."

He pulled into our driveway and held my door open for me. I was glad no one was around to see—I could have gotten into big trouble with my folks if they had known I had let him drive. Holding my hand, Derek led me to the door. It was only a few seconds, but it seemed like forever, until he said, "Well, here we are."

"Yes," I said expectantly.

Derek looked like he was debating whether to kiss me or not. Finally he just said, "Good night, Drea," and ran off to his house.

I stood by the door for a while and watched as he went inside. Naturally I was disappointed he didn't kiss me, but even so, I went to bed that night with a strange, happy feeling in my heart.

There'd be plenty of time for kissing with Derek.

Chapter Four

The rest of the family was already in the kitchen by the time I got there the following morning. It was the typical Sunday morning configuration: Mom at the kitchen table, sorting through the business section of the *Miami Herald;* Dad at the stove cooking up a batch of eggs; and Natalie impatiently waiting for the food to be served.

"Mmm, something smells wonderful," I mumbled, not yet quite awake.

"Morning, Andy," Dad said, using his special name for me. "If you can wait a minute, I'll whip you up one of my special omelets."

"Terrific," I said, pouring myself a cup of coffee at the counter.

Mom came up to me and gave me a little hug. "So you had a good time last night?"

Although I had gotten home much earlier than I had expected to, everyone was already asleep.

"How did you know?"

"Marcia called about an hour ago. She said she's never seen Derek so happy. What happened?"

Mom listened to my blow-by-blow account with rapt attention, hanging on to every word. I found it a little strange, since she never paid that close attention to any of the other dates I'd been on over the years. But then again, none of those dates had been with Derek. I had a feeling my mom had been hoping the two of us would get together.

"Are you going to go out with him again?" Natalie asked hopefully.

"Yeah," I said, taking a forkful of the omelet Dad had just set in front of me. "This is good," I added. "What's in it?"

"Thanks." He smiled at me. "It's a new recipe . . . with zucchini."

"Yecch," Natalie said. I noticed she took her eggs straight that morning.

I rummaged through the *Herald* and picked out the travel section, skimming through it for articles on Europe. One in particular, about the Mediterranean, caught my eye, and as I ate, I began to go through it.

In my sixteen and a quarter years of living, I'd yet to leave Florida. The farthest away from home I'd ever been was Disney World in Orlando, a couple of hundred miles from where I live. If I'd had anything to say about it, I'd have been all over the world by now. My big dream was to go to Europe, but the closest I'd come to convincing my parents to let me go was their requirement that first I earn at least half the cost of the trip. So far, however, I'd only managed to save $68.50 from occasional baby-sitting jobs. Still, it didn't hurt to dream.

"What's it today?" Mom asked me.

"The Mediterranean. I didn't realize all the cultures that came out of there. It sounds wonderful."

"I understand the Greek islands are beautiful," Mom said. "I bet there's interesting sea life there, too."

"All the more reason to go," I emphasized. "Maybe I could tie my trip in with some scientific expedition. Or—"

"Someday," Dad cut in. "After you get your education."

"But I'm getting my education now. I'm learning an awful lot about marine biology this year. I really like it."

"That's wonderful, Andy," Dad said. "Keep up the work, and maybe then we'll talk seriously about taking trips."

Grimacing, I finished my omelet. Why did Dad have to inject reality into my dream? It spoiled all the fun.

"I don't know why you want to bother trying to save some stupid, slimy fish, anyway," Natalie said. "It sounds like dirty work to me. Too messy."

"Just like your room," I teased.

"Is not!" she countered. "At least I don't leave all sorts of gunk in the bathroom!"

"Are you talking about my makeup?"

"That's enough, girls," Mom said in her warning voice. "Let's say we clean up these dishes, OK?"

After the dishes were put away, I went to my room, got my English notebook, then went to join my father in the family room to watch the NFL pre-game show. The Miami Dolphins were playing the Atlanta Falcons, and I didn't want to miss one minute of it. Besides, I had to write an essay on American culture for English class, and I'd decided to write mine on the football game, reasoning that I might as well pick a part of the culture I liked.

Dad was seated, as usual, in his chair and was filling up his pipe when I arrived. "I still can't believe your teacher's going to let you write about football," he said.

Perching myself comfortably on the sofa, I told him, "Mr. Kendig is interested in having us write, period. He really doesn't care what the subject is as long as we produce."

"Yeah, you could hand in a grocery list and come out with an A in his class."

I gasped at the sound of Derek's voice.

"Has the game started yet?" he asked. He was standing in the doorway, holding a glass of milk he'd helped himself to from the kitchen.

How could I have been so stupid as to forget our regular Sunday afternoon date? I thought, running my hands through my hair, which hung limply. Derek came over almost every Sunday afternoon to watch the games with us, or just with Dad if I wasn't around. I was ready to shoot myself for not having fixed myself up a bit. Between my hair and the old football shirt and jogging sweats I was wearing, I really looked a mess.

"Hi, Derek," I said, turning around, hoping he wouldn't comment on my ratty-looking appearance.

"Come in and take a seat," Dad said, smiling.

Derek plopped himself on the far end of the sofa and immediately reached over to grab some M&Ms from the candy dish on the coffee table. He looked a bit umkempt, too, like he'd just gotten out of bed or something; the T-shirt and jeans he was wearing had seen better days.

Even so, I was sure glad to see him.

"Is our bet still on?" he asked, reminding me of our weekly wagers over which team would win the Sunday game. "I say the Falcons by a touchdown."

"You're on," I said, reaching over to shake his hand.

"Don't know whether that's a wise decision," Dad told me. "The Falcons have been coming on strong this year."

"Dad, where's your loyalty?" I cried.

"Only looking at the facts, hon," he replied.

Today's game was actually a bit more important than most to Derek, and once again I mentally chided myself for having forgotten. We were both Dolphin fans, but everything changed when they played the Falcons, Derek's favorite team of all. He said it was because he liked their offense, but I had a feeling it had a lot to do with the fact that Derek's father now lived outside Atlanta and was a big Falcons fan himself. Derek said that was crazy—but even Dad thought I might have a point.

Miami won the coin toss and took first possession of the ball. I screamed with delight, predicting they'd take an early lead. But the Dolphins disappointed me, giving up the ball without even getting a first down. Atlanta didn't fare much better, and by the end of the first quarter, the score remained 0–0.

By the beginning of the second quarter, Derek had moved closer to me on the sofa. While that made me happy, at the same time I felt a little uncomfortable. Oh, not with the way I looked. I'd already gotten over that, figuring Derek liked me enough to look beyond my appearance. My discomfort had to do with Dad. Every now and again, I'd notice him looking toward us, watching to make sure we didn't do any fooling around. I tell you, the thought of even holding Derek's hand with Dad right there made me very nervous.

Derek must have been thinking the same thing, for he didn't make a move to touch me the whole time we sat there. Every time I cast my eyes toward him, though, he was there for me with a big smile. We'd just have to wait until Dad left the room, I thought.

It didn't take long for that to happen. As the game rolled into the second quarter, it took on a predictable pattern of futility on both sides. Dad began to get bored, and made the first of many trips to the refrigerator.

With Dad out of the room, I finally had Derek alone. "I wanted to tell you again what a good time I had last night."

"Me, too," Derek said, smiling, but also looking a little anxious. "I never thought dancing would be such fun."

"Especially the slow ones."

All of a sudden Derek reached over for some more M&Ms and looked very preoccupied. "Do you think we can go over our Spanish homework later? I still can't figure out the past perfect tense."

"I already did mine," I said, wondering why Derek was bringing up Spanish when Dad would be back any second.

When Dad returned with a sandwich and some drinks for us, I moved slightly away from Derek and turned my attention back to the game. I then realized that Derek had brought up Spanish for the same reason I had moved away from him—we were both uncomfortable around Dad.

I spent the rest of the game scribbling down notes for my essay, thinking all the while that the struggle going on in my mind between wanting to be close to Derek and acting as "Daddy's little girl" would have made far more interesting reading than my account of this dull game.

When the Falcons scored a field goal in the closing seconds to win the game, Derek let out a big whoop. "Way to go, boys!" he cried. Then, looking to me, he asked, "Does this even us up yet?"

"Hardly," I answered, putting aside my notebook. "If we'd bet money, I'd have made sure I won, and won enough to get to Europe and back by now. But I'm glad at least one of your teams won this weekend."

"What do you say we toss the football around a bit?" Derek asked, sounding more relaxed. "We could both use the fresh air, I think."

All I did was smile pleasantly at the thought of us being alone. We headed toward the garage, where we kept our old, battered football. Dad had bought it when I was four, hoping to turn me into south Florida's first all-state girl football star. Although that plan never quite happened, I still enjoyed just throwing the ball around.

We walked over to a nearby park, deserted now that the sun was beginning to set. Back and forth, we tossed the ball in the twilight. My tosses were fairly accurate; Derek's were neat, high spirals.

"Hey, this is almost as boring as the game," I said after a while. "I've got an idea. You throw the ball to me, and I'll try to run it by you across the sidewalk."

"You're on!" he said, ready for the challenge.

Derek didn't seem to realize that I had no intention of actually trying to make it to the pavement. I caught the ball cleanly but then I lazily ran a zigzag pattern in his direction, almost daring him to get me first.

"Hey, what are you doing?" he called from where he was standing.

"Come and get me!" I cried, holding the ball teasingly in my hand.

A little fire lit in Derek's eyes. In a flash he was there, tackling me to the ground and playfully trying to seize the ball from my arms.

We rolled around on the grass several times, Derek making a valiant play for the ball—and me loving every minute of it. But I refused to give up the ball.

Suddenly I burst into uncontrollable giggles as Derek began to tickle me. "Hey, what gives?" I squealed in between bursts.

"Give me the ball," he said playfully. "The tickle man wants the ball."

"OK," I said, surrendering. I hoped Derek would take the opportunity to continue wrestling with me, but as soon as I handed him the ball, he got up and held it in the air triumphantly.

"You fool," I said, half-upset and half-wanting him to tickle me again. "Do you think we're here just to play ball?" Catching him off guard, I tackled him around his knees and brought him back down on the ground. "Kiss me," I demanded.

"Huh?" From his reaction I could see my request was the last thing Derek had expected.

"Kiss me," I repeated.

His stunned looked gradually became a smile, and slowly he lowered his lips to mine and pressed them tight. It wasn't the most romantic kiss I'd ever had, or the most gentle. But it was from Derek, and that alone made it heavenly.

"Still want the ball?" I asked when our lips parted.

"What ball?" Derek said, looking deeply into my eyes. Then, standing, he helped me up and led me to a large palm tree at the edge of the park. "The dog-walkers won't bother us here," he said, motioning for me to sit with him under the tree.

I leaned against his strong shoulder. "I'm glad we got the chance to be alone," I whispered.

"Me, too. Your father has a very watchful eye."

"You noticed, too?"

"How could I not?" he answered. "His walking in and out of the room made me so nervous I was afraid to move. I've got to tell you, though, when I asked you to play ball with me, I wasn't thinking of this. But now that we're here I can't think of anything I'd rather be doing." He put both arms around me and then held me close for the longest time. Caressing my face with both hands, he said, "I wish I had my camera, so I could take a picture of you looking like this under the palm."

I ran my fingers through my hair. "You're kidding. I'm a mess. My hair's filthy, and my clothes—"

"Drea," he interrupted, putting his finger against my lips, "none of that. I think you look beautiful."

"You do?"

"You'd look beautiful no matter what you had on." And with that, he tackled me to the ground again and tickled me unmercifully before finally relenting with a series of hugs that left me breathless.

Chapter Five

It wasn't until the following Saturday night that Derek and I had a chance to go out again. Football practice took up most of Derek's afternoons, so he had to devote his weeknights to studying, which meant weeknight dates were out of the question.

That didn't mean I didn't see him. That week Derek began riding to school with me. I called after him Monday morning as he began to pedal away on his ten-speed, insisting he ride with me and Jane, who'd been driving me to school every day. Jane was happy to have "male blood" along, as long as Derek promised not to talk about football. Having spent most of her weekend with Randy, Jane felt she'd had enough.

I liked those morning rides with Derek. Even when neither of us had anything to say, we'd grasp each other's hands and feel love growing between us. These rides also gave Jane a chance to see that our date at the homecoming dance was no one-night stand.

That Saturday we decided to double with Jane and Randy, ending up at the nine-screen drive-in theater near the ocean. Derek sat in the backseat with me, looking handsome in what appeared to be a new blue shirt and pair of jeans.

"Derek, I didn't get a chance to congratulate you on that pass you caught last night," Jane said on the way over.

Derek, not used to compliments, seemed a little embarrassed. "It was nothing much."

"Listen to him," scoffed Randy good-naturedly. "It only changed the momentum of the game. Face it, Sebastian, you're a hero." Derek had caught a thirty-yard pass late in the fourth quarter that led to the winning touchdown. Our team won the game, 17–13.

"I couldn't have done it without your blocking," Derek answered.

"You better watch out, Sebastian," Randy said. "That kind of modesty could make you captain next year."

"Unlikely," Derek said. "I'll be just as happy if Coach Jenkins lets me start for the rest of the season. Say, you going out for basketball this year?"

"Think so. I'd like to be a sports hero, too," Randy said as he stopped at the drive-in entrance. "OK, gang, what's it going to be?"

I scanned the titles. Two of the screens were showing movies I'd already seen. Another was showing an X-rated film, and the rest featured horror movies.

"What about that one?" Derek said, pointing to the marquee listing one of the movies I'd seen, a love story.

"Didn't know you were such a romantic," Jane said. "I've already seen it, and it's dumb. Let's go to nine."

That was one of the horror movies. "Sounds fine with me," Randy agreed, heading the car toward the ticket booth. "Anyway, it doesn't really matter, folks, does it?" I saw the sly wink when he said that.

I looked at Jane and smiled. Jane had been the first one to point out to me the positive benefits of horror movies. Thanks to her expert advice, I always ended up holding hands with the boy I was with by the first scene with blood, whether I was genuinely scared or not. By the murder ,I was usually in the guy's arms, and halfway through the picture I was at the hugging stage. I had no reason to believe it would be different with Derek. The only change, as I saw it, was that I wanted to be in Derek's arms more than anything else in the world. With him it would actually mean something.

Randy and Jane went to the refreshment stand as soon as Randy parked, leaving Derek and me alone in the backseat. "You know, Drea, I'm really surprised at you," he said after they left.

"What do you mean?"

"I didn't know you liked horror movies. I thought you couldn't stand the sight of blood."

"That's true," I said. "But who said anything about looking at it?" Derek hadn't yet been exposed to the "plan," but it wouldn't take long for him to see what I meant.

"Who wants popcorn?" Randy opened his door just then and handed us a big tubful. Jane was carrying a tray of soft drinks.

"Sit back, folks," Randy said, climbing back into the car. "We're about to be entertained."

Derek whispered in my ear. "If it gets too gory for you, just hold on to me."

"I will, Derek."

The movie began soon after that. The plot was really twisted, something about a crazed war hero going berserk on Veteran's Day. I couldn't ask either Jane or Randy about it because as soon as the opening credits appeared, they were in each other's arms, hugging. They didn't waste any time, I thought, but then again they'd been dating each other for close to four months.

Derek, on the other hand, was actually watching the movie at first. He was stretched out over three-quarters of the backseat, his head resting on the top of the seat close to mine. But he made no move to "comfort" me, other than grabbing my right hand firmly. His other hand just as firmly grasped the tub of popcorn in his lap.

At one point the only sound in the car was the chomp-chomp of his eating. "Say, what's that noise back there?" Jane asked from the front.

I could see I had to put the plan into action. "Derek, I'm scared," I whispered. The crazed killer had just taken his first victim.

Derek turned to face me. "Sorry," he whispered, maneuvering an arm around my shoulders and giving me a quick squeeze, then taking his arm away. "Have some popcorn. Does wonders for soothing the nerves."

"If you insist," I said, reaching for a handful. The second time I moved my hand to the tub, I let it rest for a moment on his. That was enough of a hint for Derek. He put the popcorn on the floor and put his arm around me.

We sat like that for the rest of the movie. It felt really comforting and nice to snuggle with Derek like that—even if we didn't kiss. At one point in the movie the whole screen seemed to explode with blood, and I gave up and simply buried my face in his chest. Derek rubbed my shoulder soothingly and whispered in my ear that everything was all right.

"Thanks, hon," I whispered to his heart.

Derek straightened up. "What did you call me?"

I had to think a moment. What *did* I say? "Hon. I guess it just came out."

"I like that," he whispered, pulling me a little closer. "What should I call you?"

"Whatever you want," I answered. "Whatever feels comfortable."

He thought for a moment. "How about kitten?"

I made a face. Cats were never one of my favorite animals. "Do you really think of me like that?"

He moved his hand even closer. "No, it's just the first thing that came to mind." After a while he said, "Well, dear sounds too old, and babe is too—oh, just not right. How about just Drea for now."

Smiling, I said, "I like that just fine."

"At the risk of offending our friends in the front seat, I've got to say I can't wait until I get my license. I think I'd rather be alone with you."

"I know what you mean." So he felt more comfortable kissing me when we were alone. I sighed with relief.

After the movie Randy and Jane dropped us off at my house, and Derek walked me up to the front door. We seemed to be frozen for the next few moments. As I stood there waiting for Derek to kiss me, he shuffled his feet back and forth as if debating his next move. Then, suddenly, without any warning, he raised my head to his with his fingers and pressed his lips to mine.

It wasn't anything like I'd imagined. This kiss, which I'd been waiting for all night long, felt exactly like the watery, fumbling attempt it was. Even though it was Derek, I was incredibly surprised at how little I enjoyed it.

Struggling to hide my disappointment, I pulled back and smiled. "Good night, Derek," I said. "It's getting late."

Thank goodness all Derek saw was my smile. "Good night, Drea," he answered, planting another small, wet kiss on my nose. "Sweet dreams."

"See you tomorrow," I added, as I watched him walk over the grass to his house. Yes, tomorrow, I thought hopefully. Maybe then we could try again—and make it feel the way it was supposed to.

Chapter Six

Saturday, December 6, I was planted in the kitchen, my elbows deep in unbleached flour and egg whites. Following a recipe from one of my mother's cookbooks, I was attempting to bake my first layer cake. I was taking my time—this was one cake that had to be perfect.

It was Derek's birthday cake.

Derek's birthday was actually Monday, but by mutual agreement we'd decided to celebrate on Saturday. His mom was away that weekend visiting her sister in Tampa, and so we had the run of Derek's house.

I had the whole thing planned down to the last detail. Our very own private birthday party. I'd bring the cake over later in the afternoon, at which time I'd begin preparations for dinner.

Derek and I had been dating about six weeks now, and I decided that he was the most thoughtful, enjoyable boyfriend I'd ever had. The possibility of dating anyone else was out of the question—in fact, when Roger tried to get me back two weeks after he dumped me, I was only too pleased to turn him away by announcing that I belonged to one Derek Sebastian.

Once football season was over, Derek had a lot more time to spend with me. Often we'd meet at his house for a night of Pac-Man (my favorite) or Missile Command (his favorite). Or we'd walk around the curved streets of our neighborhood at twilight, holding hands and talking about nothing in particular. He finally did get that photograph of me under the palm tree—in fact, he got a whole series of them, which he plastered up in his bedroom right next to his photos of Charlene Tilton, Pat Benatar, and Reggie Jackson.

"I don't know how you did it," I told him when he showed me the photos for the first time. "I hardly recognize this girl."

"I didn't do anything special, Drea. All I did was capture the love in your eyes."

"No, Derek, it's more than that," I said. "You can really do things with that camera. Maybe you should take pictures for the school paper or shoot weddings and stuff."

"Aw, any idiot can handle a camera," he scoffed.

"Oh, yeah?" I picked up the camera off his dresser, hastily pointed it in his direction, and snapped the shutter. "I'll bet that picture will be blurry. I can't handle this thing."

"You're right about that," Derek said, trying to keep a straight face. "There's no film in this camera, dummy!" With that, he took the camera from my hand and gave me a big kiss.

But there lay the only problem in our relationship—his kisses. I still hadn't been able to get anything from him but those short, slightly off-the-mark, closed-lip kisses. The truth was, I hadn't mustered up enough courage to tell him they weren't doing anything for me. I still kept hoping that the next one, or the one after it, would do the trick. But if anything, they only seemed to get worse.

I knew I'd go out of my mind, however, if this kept up, and that was why I was going all out on this little celebration. Tonight was the night, I determined, that I'd get the the bottom of the situation once and for all.

I grabbed the pan of melted chocolate and slowly poured it into the batter. The cake was a devil's-food, Derek's favorite. Making the cake was a big part of the plan, too. I'd read somewhere how chocolate is supposed to make a person feel real romantic, and judging from my own experience with brownies, I felt there might be some truth to that. So far, the batter looked the way batter was supposed to, and with some degree of satisfaction, I finished mixing it up, then transferred it into the baking pans, and put the pans in the oven.

"Something smells good," Natalie said, walking through the back door.

"It's Derek's birthday cake, and you can't have any," I told her.

"Boy, you never make anything for me anymore. Everything is Derek, Derek, Derek."

"Sorry," I said. "But it's time you learned how to make your own."

"Maybe I will," she said, smiling slyly. "See, I've got someone to bake for now."

"Oh, really?" I said, amazed.

"Jonathan Cooper danced with me three times at the school dance last night." Natalie opened the refrigerator and took out a container of yogurt. "He says I'm cute."

"Congratulations," I said. I wondered what Mom would say about Natalie's new find. She didn't let me go out on dates until I was thirteen.

"Maybe if I can get Jonathan to ask me on a real date, we can double sometime. I'd love to see you do it with Derek."

"Get out of here!" I said playfully, ready to fling a dish towel at her. That was the last thing in the the world I needed.

After taking the cake tins out of the oven and setting the layers on racks to cool, I went to get ready for my "date" with Derek. Earlier that week, when I had bought the cologne I'd be giving him for his birthday, I'd picked up some for myself as well. It was a new fragrance I'd seen advertised in a magazine, one that promised to "drive the man in your life wild." I also bought a new eye pencil, and now I carefully ringed the color around my eyes, making their deep blue color really stand out. Together with my bouncy short hair, my appearance was definitely catlike—much as I hated to admit to that image. But I was pleased with the look and was convinced Derek would be, too.

Back at the kitchen I put the finishing touches on the cake. I whipped up some chocolate icing and carefully iced the cake. Using a tube of blue cake-decorating gel, I made a swirling border on the top of the icing. Then in the middle, holding my hand steady so it wouldn't shake, I inscribed the words *I Love You, Derek* with the neat penmanship that had earned me an A in grade school. He's gonna love this, I told myself.

That was a bit of an understatement. "This is fantastic!" he shouted when I showed him the cake. "You made this from scratch—just for me?"

"Just wait till you taste it," I said. "The best."

"What are we waiting for?"

"Not so fast. This is for dessert. You've got to sit through my meal first."

"What is it?"

"Your favorite. Spaghetti and meatballs. With garlic bread."

"Where is it?"

"At the store. And you're coming with me. Let's go."

We borrowed my mother's car for the trip to the Winn-Dixie, where I picked up all the ingredients for the meal. I can't even remember how many times our mothers sent us down here, on our bikes, for one thing or another over the years. But this trip with Derek was something else. For once we were shopping for ourselves, like we were grown-up and on our own. And it did make me feel grown-up, choosing the items, comparing brands and prices. For a little while I even pretended Derek and I were married and that we were stocking our honeymoon apartment with provisions.

"Care to fill me in on your little secret?" Derek asked, noticing the gleam in my eyes at the thought of us together forever.

I was a little embarrassed. "No," I told him. I picked up a can of tomato sauce and pretended to read the label.

"I thought we had no secrets." Derek took the can from my hand and put it in our cart.

"A woman is entitled to some secrets," I countered. "A man, too, for that matter. Anyway, forget it. It's nothing important."

"I've got a secret. I was just walking down these aisles remembering all the times we've done this before and thinking how funny it would be if we were still shopping here when we're a couple of old folks and—"

My laugh made him stop.

"It's not that funny," he said.

"That was sort of like what I was thinking," I said, still giggling.

Derek put his arm around me. "C'mon. Let's get the birthday boy back home."

As I stood in the Sebastian kitchen and prepared dinner, the image of being Mrs. Derek Sebastian kept popping into my head. As much as the thought pleased me—what girl wouldn't be proud to have a guy like Derek as a husband someday?—I was plagued by one nagging doubt: Could I ever marry someone who gave me sloppy kisses?

Derek had a bit of a surprise for me when I went into the dining room to set up the table. He'd beaten me to it, having taken out his mother's best china and set it on what appeared to be her best tablecloth. Two candlesticks were centered on the table, the candles already lit.

"How romantic," I whispered.

When we got down to eating, I regretted not having made another dish. "Next time I do this I'm not going to make spaghetti," I said.

"Why not? It's delicious," Derek said, twisting some strands onto his fork.

"I forgot that every time I eat this I feel like a horse nibbling from the trough." To emphasize my point I sucked a few sauce-laden pieces into my mouth. "Hardly romantic-looking, huh?"

"Doesn't matter to me," Derek said. "In fact, it makes you look adorable."

"Bet you say that to all the girls," I teased. I couldn't wait until we were finished eating and could get on with the real purpose of the evening.

Feeling stuffed but heavenly, I pushed myself away from the table, took the dirty dishes into the kitchen, and brought out the cake with sixteen candles, plus one for good luck, perched on top.

"Make a wish," I told him before he blew them out. He had no trouble extinguishing them all in one breath.

"What'd you wish?" I asked eagerly.

Derek gave me one of those what-are-you-stupid-or-something looks. "You know I can't tell you. It won't come true then."

"You're right," I admitted.

"I'll tell you I wish we had another cake. I like what this one says too much to want to cut it up."

"There's more of that where it came from," I said. "I love you, Derek. Happy birthday." Standing up, I bent over and gave him a kiss.

"I love you too, Drea." I could see the truth of the words in his eyes.

I gave him the cologne then, along with a leather keychain with the words *Happiness is having a friend like you* embossed on it. Derek loved the gifts, and after he transferred his keys to the new ring, he got up and led me into the living room, lit only by the reflected light from the adjacent dining room. "Have a seat." He pointed to the sofa and set me down on its edge, seating himself right next to me.

"You've made this the happiest birthday of my life," he said.

"I'm so glad you feel that way, Der. I've waited a long time for this."

"I know. It's taken me a while to grow up. You always were ahead of me."

"Not anymore," I added.

Derek pushed his lips on mine. I wish I could describe a more romantic or gentle kiss, but the truth was that all I could feel were Derek's teeth pushing against the layers of our rigid lips. Uncontrollably I stiffened and pulled away.

"Something wrong?" Derek leaned back.

The concern in his voice, coupled with the darkness of the room, gave me the courage to speak. "We have no secrets, right?" I began.

"Well, this afternoon you said—"

"Never mind that. Derek, I—um—I've got to tell you something. . . . You kiss funny."

"Huh?"

"Let me take that back—that doesn't sound right."

"You bet it doesn't sound right." He stood up and walked to the window facing the street.

"I'm sorry, Derek. Let me explain."

"Sure, what you mean is, I'm not as good as

the other guys, huh? Don't measure up." He sounded defeated and defensive.

"That's not true," I said. "I love you, Derek, and I know you love me, too. It's just that as far as kissing goes, well, you're just new at it. All you need is a little practice." I walked up to him and put my arms around his waist.

"I thought six weeks counted for more than practice."

"It's hard for me to talk about it. I knew you'd take it personally—"

"How else am I supposed to take it!" he cried, pulling away from my grasp.

I took a deep breath and said quietly, "Please, let me explain. What I think of your kissing has nothing to do with how I feel about you. I just want to make it better for both of us."

"I bet you're sorry you ever went out with me."

"Derek, that's nonsense! I love you—and you know that."

Hearing those words, he seemed to soften, and he turned around.

"Hear me out. All I mean is, you've been stiff when you kiss. You should relax, let your lips loosen, like this." I puckered my lips and softly touched them on his. I felt no resistance on his end, which was good because at that moment I was afraid I'd made him real mad.

"See what I mean?" I said after demonstrating the kind of kiss I wanted.

"Wow, that was something." He gasped, and at that moment I realized he'd probably never been kissed that way by any other girl. He truly didn't know what he'd been missing. "Let me try."

He turned back to me and kissed me again. This time he was a little more secure, a little more relaxed. I, in turn, relaxed and draped my arms around him.

"I can't breathe," he said after about ten seconds of this.

"The secret, Derek, is in turning your head at a slight angle to mine. That way there's room for you to breathe. Like this." Again we kissed, and this time it was better still.

"I can get used to this," Derek said, getting more comfortable and gaining more confidence with each passing moment. "Let's do it again."

By the end of the night, Derek was kissing like the best of them and I could have kicked myself for having wasted all this time.

Chapter Seven

"Could you repeat that, Derek? You're not making any sense." The phone line was clear as a bell, but Derek was going on like a madman.

"I'm getting a car!" This time he said it so I could understand. "Dad sent me the money for my birthday."

"I can't believe it!" I shouted into the phone.

"Think of how I feel. I didn't even expect a card from him. Let alone this."

"Does your mom know?"

"I called her at the store as soon as I got the letter. She thinks it's great. She said it was the least he could do for me after all these years."

I knew exactly what he meant. Derek's father had not been the most devoted of fathers since he left Florida and Derek's mother behind. "Have you thought about what kind you're getting?"

"I thought I'd go over to Littleton's and see what they've got hanging around."

"I have a better idea. Why don't we wait till Dad gets home and ask him for some advice? He knows cars."

"You think he would have time?" Derek asked eagerly.

"Do you have to ask? Of course he would."

Not only did Dad agree to help Derek with his car selection, but he pored over car magazines with us, and the following night he took us car shopping. By the end of the week, Derek found what he wanted, a sporty muscle car that was several years old but in good working order.

"I'm a pretty fair mechanic, Derek," Dad said as Derek drove us back to his house. "I can show you how to keep this baby running if you want."

"Thanks a lot, Mr. Mallory." Derek smiled. "I'll need the help. In the meantime, I have another request. I'd like to take your daughter for a drive."

"OK, Dad?" I asked eagerly.

"Sure. Just don't be late for dinner."

Like an experienced driver, Derek took off down our quiet street. Once we got onto the highway, he glided in and out of traffic like a snake. "All those hours of playing Night Driver paid off, I think," he told me.

"Just be careful," I warned. The last thing I wanted was to see Derek wreck the car the first day he had it.

But while Derek drove a little too fast for my

taste, he remained very careful and sure of himself the whole time we were in the car. The most infuriating part was that he refused to tell me where we were going. All he said was, "It's a surprise." And I mean that was all.

When we stopped at a light, he explained that he could concentrate better if he didn't have to talk while he drove. "But you can listen to my stereo." He pointed proudly to the stereo cassette player that came with the car.

Derek came to a stop when we reached the beach, pulling in at a deserted parking lot. "Let's go." He opened the door on my side and, taking my hand, let me out.

The beach was deserted as well as the parking lot, and I could see we were heading for the little breakwater at the edge of the ocean, the secret place I'd wanted to go after the homecoming dance.

"Surprised?" Derek asked as we made our way to the rocky spot.

"Not really," I answered. "I knew sooner or later you'd remember the times we used to spend here."

"I never forgot. This place has been on my mind ever since you agreed to go out with me. But I wanted to be able to drive you here on my own."

"It's been worth the wait. I love this spot."

Derek's face darkened. "You've never been here with other guys, have you?"

"You're the only person I'd want to share this spot with," I whispered close to his ear.

Taking my hand, he guided me up on the rocks. The waves were rocking the shore right below us, their gentle rhythm making a peaceful, lulling backdrop for our conversation. I'd been here often by myself, to think and to dream, but it took on a whole new dimension with Derek next to me. It was much better than I had imagined.

"Do you remember the day we first found this place?" I asked as we sat and watched the changing colors in the late afternoon sky.

"Uh-huh. As I recall, you were into shells and refused to go home until you found a conch."

"But I did—right here," I added. "Too bad you hardly see any around here anymore."

"We could look," Derek suggested, turning to face me. "But let's not right now." He reached out and touched my hair. "I love you, Drea," he whispered softly.

"I love you, too, Derek. I always have, you know."

Any further words were stopped by the kiss we both felt we needed to share. We held it for the longest time, our heads ever so close, our souls as close as two people's could be. After our lips parted, there was no need for words—even if I tried, I couldn't have come close to describing the love I felt for Derek at that moment.

Sighing, I rested my head against Derek's strong chest and looked at the water, now navy blue against the darkening sky. "It's beautiful, isn't it?"

"They say everything is beautiful when you're in love," Derek said.

"Whoever 'they' are, they're absolutely right," I agreed. "I always feel so free when I come here." I sighed peacefully. "Sometimes when I look out there, I realize how much of the world there is to see."

"What do you need the world for?" Derek asked impatiently. "There's so much here right now."

"I'm not talking about us. That's special, and no one can take that away. I'm talking about something beyond our relationship."

"Like what?"

"Like life itself. There's so much to do out there," I said, pointing to the ocean.

"I don't see anything but water," he quipped.

"I'm serious, Derek. Even in the ocean, there is a whole world I'd like to explore. Just imagine how exciting it would be to save the whales or to rescue little baby seals from the hunters. But I was thinking, too, about all the things that exist beyond this little area we live in. Aren't you curious about what's there?"

"I suppose," he said, without much enthusiasm. "But what's wrong with what's here?"

"Nothing's wrong. But it's . . . limited."

Derek turned away. "Am I limited?"

"Oh, Derek, I told you this had nothing to do with us. And you should know more than anyone how much I want to see for myself what's out there. I've talked about it for ages."

Derek picked up a stone and threw it far out into the ocean. "This part of the world is enough for me now." I watched the stone hit the water.

"Bet I can throw one farther," I said, to change the subject. I didn't like it when Derek and I disagreed, especially here. It put a gulf between us that left me uncomfortable. Maybe I could change his mind about the world, open his up to the possibilities that were out there for both of us. After all, I'd taught him so much already.

I picked up a stone and threw it as far as I could.

"Don't think it went as far as mine," Derek said. "But not bad for a girl."

"Oh, yeah?" I challenged, laughing. This time I stood up and hurled the stone a good hundred feet or so into the foamy white water. "Top that!" I said, turning to face him smugly.

But Derek wasn't up for it. "Let's not compete against each other. It's against my nature. Come back here."

As soon as I sat back down, he grabbed me in his arms and held me close. "I love you, Drea," he whispered hoarsely. "Don't ever leave me."

"I won't, ever," I said, kissing him. Right then I felt so secure, so loved in a very special way, that I filed my dreams of travel in the back of my mind.

The sky was dark by the time Derek sped me back home. I hoped I wouldn't be late for dinner. I knew my parents would be mad if I was—even if I was with Derek.

Fortunately, I walked in the door just as Mom was setting the roast beef on the table. It was just Mom, Dad, and me tonight—Natalie was spending the night at her friend Wendy's. Quickly I washed up, sat at my seat, and dug silently into the food.

"Well, Andy," Dad said after a while. "Derek's car run well?"

"Wonderful, Dad," I answered, stuffing a piece of meat in my mouth. "And you'd be proud of the way he drives, too."

"That's good to hear." He smiled. "Say, Drea, how are you two getting along?"

Mom looked at Dad in amazement. "Do you even have to ask? I've never seen our little girl happier, have you?"

"We're getting along just fine, Dad," I answered. "Why do you ask?"

"I don't want to see either of you hurt," he replied darkly.

"Who said anything about getting hurt? Derek and I have a very special relationship." I dug determinedly into my string beans.

"I hope you're right, dear," Dad said. But the look of worry remained on his face. "Sixteen just seems a little too young for 'very special relationships.' "

"Dad, you're sounding just like Jane did when Derek and I first started going out. Or do you know something I don't know?" This afternoon Derek seemed to make his feelings for me quite clear, but I also knew that Derek confided things to my dad that he wouldn't tell anyone else—even me.

"Nothing specific, Andy. Just that people your age do a lot of growing very quickly. I'd hate for either one of you to put too much into this relationship that may not be there."

Dad was talking in circles, but the dark tone he used made me feel queasy. Unconsciously I twirled my fork around the plate, the string beans making a dizzying whirlpool around it.

"Now look what you've done, Rick," Mom scolded. "Getting Andrea all upset over nothing." To me she said, "Never mind your father. I'm sure you have nothing to worry about. Now finish up your dinner, dear."

"I'm not so hungry anymore," I said. "I think I'll go to my room now." Tossing my napkin on my plate, I got up and left the table.

"I really do worry about those two," I could hear Dad say faintly from the hallway.

"They're just kids," Mom told him. "Let them have their fun."

Thanks, Mom, I said to myself. I was glad one of my parents, at least, knew the score. But it was just like Dad to give me a warning like that. Always the realist, he wanted to make sure I knew both the dark and the light sides of a situation—even if it meant spoiling what had been a perfect afternoon with Derek.

Despite his warning, I knew I had nothing to worry about. Just one look around my room let me know that Derek still was and always would be a very important part of my life. One of the first things I saw when I shut my door assured me of that—my autographed poster of Bucky Dent, a little faded now but still tacked on to the back of my bedroom door. Derek was with me when I got Bucky's signature—the most momentous event of my twelfth year. In fact, it was Derek who brought me to the Yankees spring training camp to get my poster signed. We both missed school that day to go out to the camp, and we both had to pay for it later, but the great time we had further cemented our friendship and made our punishment of being grounded seem worth it.

On my desk I still had the scorecard from the time Derek and I took Natalie miniature golfing. I was baby-sitting her, and Derek came along—to make sure no big boys bothered us, he said. We were around thirteen, but you would have thought Derek was twenty from the masterful way he chose our clubs and led us around the mini course. The only time he seemed to weaken was when I scored two holes-in-one in a row. Then I thought he would quit in frustration, but no, he bravely held on—for Natalie's sake, I think—and even treated us to Cokes afterward. A gallant display of good sportsmanship, I thought.

I couldn't help but love a guy like that. And I felt so lucky he'd chosen me to be his girl.

Chapter Eight

Around seven o'clock on Christmas morning, I met Derek on the strip of grass that separated our houses. We had picked this spot to exchange our presents because we wanted to be alone, for even at this early hour, both of our houses were buzzing with the frenetic activity of the holiday.

I felt a bittersweet tenderness as I waited for Derek to arrive. This would be the last time I'd see him for a week—our first separation since we'd begun dating. In less than two hours he'd be catching a plane to Atlanta, where he'd spend the rest of the vacation with his father. He wasn't too happy about going, but with his father giving him the car and all, he felt he must.

We planned to make this meeting short, since we had spent lots of time saying our goodbyes in heartfelt kisses as Christmas arrived the night before. I tried not to think about what the vacation would be like without him around, dwelling instead on all the things we'd be doing together once he got back. Still, I couldn't help but let a tear or two fall, realizing that Derek would be so far away when I wanted—and needed—him around most.

I looked up to see Derek coming my way, handsome in a green, cotton-knit shirt that brought out the sparkle in his eyes. "Hey, no one's supposed to cry on Christmas," he said.

"Oh, I just got something in my eye," I shot back quickly.

"You can't fool me," he said, brushing the wetness from my cheeks. "Don't worry, I'll be back in a week, and I promise to write every day. I'm not exactly thrilled about going either."

"I know," I said. "But it doesn't change things."

"Think of it this way. Look at all the time you'll have to get your marine biology report done."

"Who cares about that? I'd rather be with you."

"And I'd rather be with you. But maybe this can serve as a reminder." Derek handed me a small, square-shaped box wrapped in silver paper.

I handed Derek my presents to him. "These should keep you occupied on the trip up."

Derek opened his first: a book on auto repair I knew he wanted and some filters for his camera. "Hey, these are terrific," he said, dropping the boxes to thank me with a kiss and hug. "Open yours now."

Inside the small box was a gorgeous silver band with a very interesting pattern on it that I couldn't quite make out.

Derek noticed my confusion. "The pattern reminded me a lot of the ocean."

"It's beautiful, Derek. I love it. And it does kind of look like waves, doesn't it?" I took the ring out of the box and placed it on my ring finger. It fit perfectly.

"I thought you'd like it for that reason."

"I do. Oh, Derek, I love you so much."

"I love you too, Drea."

Tenderly we embraced each other, and the passion I felt for Derek washed over me like waves from a hurricane. I didn't want to let go of him at all, but we drew apart at Mrs. Sebastian's call.

"I've got to go now." Derek gave me one last kiss on the nose and then slowly backpedaled toward his house.

"Hurry back, you bozo," I cried, " 'cause I'm missing you already." I ran back to the house, through the kitchen door, without once turning back. I knew I'd really start to cry if I did.

Chapter Nine

In a way I was lucky that Derek left for Atlanta on Christmas. With everyone at home and Christmas presents still to exchange, I had plenty to do to keep myself from dwelling on his absence. Mom's holiday music, which she insisted on playing every year, filled the entire house, and to my surprise it kept me feeling happy and festive all day long. I have to thank my family, too, for seeing to it that I didn't have the opportunity to be alone at all throughout the day. Dad gave Mom a video camera, and Natalie insisted I take pictures of her opening up her many gifts. Then, after viewing herself on the TV, she begged me to show her how she could cover up the tiny pimples on her face, which, admittedly, looked pretty unsavory when viewed close up.

At first I wasn't too crazy about the idea, but soon I got caught up in Natalie's curiosity about make overs. Natalie was a very patient and willing model, so after I nearly poked out her eye with the mascara wand, she gave me a second chance at smoothing out her skin with my cover-up and adding a touch of color to her cheeks and lips. By the time I finished, I found myself with a potential beauty on my hands. I looked positively dowdy by comparison.

"Jonathan Cooper won't be able to resist you now," I said emphatically.

But Natalie just sighed. "I don't think it's enough. Ever since basketball season started, he hasn't even noticed I'm alive."

"Never underestimate the power of the makeup kit."

"I thought you were always trying to tell me that beauty doesn't mean anything."

She's got me on that one, I thought. "Well, what I mean is that beauty isn't *everything*. But it doesn't hurt to try to look your best."

"I don't know, Drea," Natalie said, turning away from the bathroom sink and returning to our bedroom. "It took you over an hour to put all this junk on me. That seems like too much time to waste on a boy."

"You get faster as you go along. You never see me slaving over my makeup, do you?"

"That's because you've got Derek. You don't have to."

"Are you implying I don't look as good as I could?"

"All I know is that you used to spend hours in front of the mirror before your dates with—um—that guy you went with before Derek."

"Roger. I did?"

"Uh-huh." Natalie folded her arms across her chest for emphasis.

"Well, if I did, it was because *all* Roger was interested in was looks. He's a very shallow boy, and I hope you never get involved with anyone like him. With Derek, looks are secondary. Of course I do my best to look nice for him, but we have lots more important things to deal with when we're together."

"Like what?" she asked eagerly.

"Things you're too young to know about," I said, closing the subject.

But Natalie's comment got me to thinking about the way I treated Derek. Had I taken him so for granted that I neglected my looks? Somehow I didn't think so, but I made a mental note to pay more attention to my appearance the next time I saw him.

I spent the rest of my vacation dividing time between schoolwork and friends. I hadn't realized how much time Derek had been taking out of my life until the day I went shopping with Jane. We hadn't spent an entire day together in months, and, believe me, I had a great time. We cracked ourselves up trying on wigs in a department store and looking through every stack of records in the mall record shop for an obscure album Jane had heard on the radio the night before. We didn't find it, but we did find a record that had nothing but people laughing on it, and on impulse I bought it. We laughed so hard when I played it at home, I thought we were going to die.

"How come we don't do this more often?" I asked her later, when we were listening to more normal sounds on the radio.

Jane's answer was simple. "The boys. Sometimes they make us forget we ever did things with other girls."

"But when I'm with Derek, I never think about doing things like this."

"That's the point. I'd be less than truthful if I said you were at the top of my mind when I'm with Randy. But it doesn't make you any less of a friend."

"I wish there was a way we could all do things together. Besides double dates, I mean."

Jane leaned back on Natalie's headboard. "Maybe there is. You know the Student Follies?"

"Who doesn't? It's only the cultural highlight of the school year," I said sarcastically.

"Well, I was talking with Margo David yesterday, and she said she's trying to gather a bunch of couples to work up an act for the show. You interested?"

"Could be fun," I mused. "I'd be interested, but I'm afraid I don't sing too well."

"Neither does anyone else. But there's something amusing about being in a group that makes a total fool of itself. That, my dear, is the essence of the follies."

"Then I'll answer for Derek and sign us up."

"If you're game, Randy and I'll go along, too. I'll pass the word to Margo when I see her."

That night I wrote to Derek, telling him all about the possibility of appearing in the follies. I was joking about its being a "cultural" event, but it actually was one of the biggest events of the school year. For some people it was a chance to show off their talents—the school bands and choirs always played a big part in it, as well as some truly talented singers and dancers. But for the rest of us, it was a chance to play star for a night and have a good time. I hoped Derek wouldn't mind my saying he would participate.

Fingering the ring he gave me, I tried to visualize his expression the moment he read the letter. Wearing this ring made me feel closer than ever to Derek; he'd picked the most perfect thing to give me to make me feel truly that I was his girl.

Then I thought, why don't I call him?

Before he left, he had written down the number for me on a scrap of paper. I grabbed the piece of paper from my desk and ran to the extension in my parents' bedroom. I picked up the phone and dialed. Unfortunately, the woman on the other end of the line told me in a clipped voice that Derek wasn't there. So I just left a message for him to please call me back.

For the rest of the evening, I kept an ear out for the phone, jumping like a scared rabbit the two times it rang. But neither call was from Derek, and I went to bed that night feeling terribly disappointed.

I received his first letter on December 29, four days after he left. As I feared, he wasn't getting along too well with his father, and the letter left me slightly depressed. I wanted things to be so right for Derek. There was no mention, either, of my call to him, and I began to wonder if he ever even received the message.

On a brighter note, Derek was right about one thing—this vacation was the perfect opportunity for me to make significant progress on my marine biology report. It was due the second week in January, and I knew if I wanted to get a good grade on it, I had to finish the paper—or at least almost finish it—before vacation was over.

In my paper I planned to explore the effects of pollution on southern Florida fish, and for research I went down to the county library, which had an extensive reference section on the subject. For three days I camped out at the table closest to that section, spreading books and magazines around me as if they were my fortress against the world. I found the information fascinating, much more than I had imagined it would be before I started the project. I wished that Derek were around, to share this with me.

On my third day there, I was searching the shelves only to discover that the book I wanted was in the hands of a tall, masculine body standing next to me.

"Sam?" I whispered to the boy, whom I recognized from class. "What are you doing here?"

Sam smiled back, his twinkling blue eyes shining through his wire-frame glasses. "Same as you, I imagine. Working on my report."

"Stupid question on my part. That book you're holding is the one I'm looking for."

Sam quickly scanned the index before handing it to me. "All yours. But if I were you, I'd put it back. Most of the information is outdated."

I looked surprised. "How do you know that?"

Sam motioned to follow him back to the table, where we both sat down. "I just spent the past week at the University of Miami. Their marine biology department has all the latest information in the field."

"Hmm, I didn't know you were so interested."

Sam self-consciously combed his fingers through his sandy blond hair. "To tell you the truth, I wasn't until Billings's class. He really made it come to life for me."

"Really? Me, too!"

I must have said that too loudly, for the next sound I heard was a big "shhh!" from the librarian. "Whoops," I whispered. "Say, what's your report on?"

"The Save the Whales movement. I really admire what those people are doing."

"So do I," I said.

"I wish Billings would spend more time on stuff like that than on the mating cycle of some obscure freshwater fish. I think it's a lot more important."

"Well, I understand why we need to know about basic biology, but I know what you mean. I've even given some thought to someday working with one of the preservationist organizations. Some of the information I've uncovered for my report is pretty scary."

"If you're really interested, I seriously hope you do something about it. Let me tell you. . . ."

For about a half hour Sam held my attention with the facts he'd learned about the whales. I was impressed with his findings and glad to have discovered another person in the class who shared my enthusiasm for the field. No one else seemed to care.

"Well, Sam, I'd really like to hear more about your report when you get done," I told him.

"Tell you what. I've got some books at home you might be interested in. What do you say we discuss them tonight over a pizza at Sal's? Maybe we can even catch a movie afterward."

I didn't answer for a second. The question, so abrupt and from such an unlikely source as

Sam, struck me dumb with shock. "I can't, Sam," I told him when I found my voice. "I'm dating Derek Sebastian, and he wouldn't like it."

"But would you?" he asked pointedly.

"No," I answered quickly. "Derek means too much to me to go out with anyone else. But thanks for asking—and I would like to read your report when it's done."

"Suit yourself," he said, rising. "See you in class."

Sam seemed so insulted I felt I had to say something. "Sam," I said as he began to walk off. "See you around."

"Drea, is that you?" Derek shouted over the long-distance line. "The connection's so bad I can hardly hear you."

"I hear you loud and clear," I answered, relieved that Derek was able to get through. The clock read 11:57; in three minutes it would be a new year.

"I've been trying to call since eleven-thirty—the circuits have been busy. I never realized what a busy place Seminole Grove is."

"It's so good to hear your voice, Derek. I miss you so much."

"I miss you, too. It's been miserable without you. I'm sorry I never called you back—I never knew you called until you wrote me about it. Dad's wife's not too good at leaving messages."

"From your letters I gather it hasn't been such a good vacation for you."

"The worst. I'll be so glad to get home. I figure I'll be back just in time to watch the Orange Bowl with you."

"Terrific!" I cried. "What have you been doing tonight?"

"Dad and his wife are throwing a party. If you hear any noise in the background, that's it. But it's all old people—a real drag. What are you doing?"

"Margo and Jesse invited me to a party, but I didn't want to go without you. Spending this time with you is more important than going out anywhere," I said. "So I've been listening to WYFY's countdown of the year's hits."

"Just like we used to do when we were kids."

"I know." I didn't tell Derek, but that was the very reason I put the station on in the first place. Listening to the songs with snapshots I had of Derek in front of me made him seem much closer.

A burst of sound made Derek's next words barely audible. Then I realized it was midnight and the new year was upon us.

"Happy new year!" Derek shouted into the phone.

"Happy new year!" I shouted back. "I love you, Derek."

"I love you too, Drea. Dad's motioning me to get off the phone now. I'll see you tomorrow."

* * *

As the skies darkened over Seminole Grove the following evening, I rose from the sofa, where I'd spent the entire day watching bowl games with Dad, and went to my room. Remembering Natalie's admonition at Christmas, I took off my sweatshirt and jeans, showered, and then put on my off-white sweater dress.

This is really going to surprise Derek, I pleasantly dreamed. The dress emphasized my improving body and that, in combination with my knockout cologne and new lipstick, assured me I'd be presenting him with the best possible welcome-home present—a new me.

Still, I wasn't prepared for the looks I got from my own family when I entered the den. "Drea, I can't believe it's you," Dad said, his pipe nearly dropping from his opened jaw.

"You look magnificent," Mom complimented, putting her needlepoint aside to get up and straighten out the lines of my dress. "What's the occasion?"

"Derek'll be coming over as soon as he gets back. It's a surprise for him."

Natalie whistled approvingly. "I'll say."

About an hour later Derek appeared, holding a bunch of carnations he picked up for me at the airport. "My welcome-home present to you," he said, hugging me in a friendly bearlike vise.

After a few minutes of welcoming hugs and remarks, during which time he never once acknowledged my appearance, we sat down to watch the game. It was so good to have Derek sitting next to me that my displeasure at him for failing to notice my dress rapidly went away. By the time the second quarter began, it was as if he'd never been gone. Now that he was home, the more pleasant events of his trip began to surface, and he entertained me with lots of stories of the people he met and places he visited with his father.

In the closing minutes of the game, Derek finally acknowledged the dress. "Drea, I have to admit you really threw me with that outfit. It's the last thing I ever imagined to see on you."

"Does it bother you?"

"No," he said slowly. "I just didn't expect it. And it kind of puts a crimp in my plans for after the game."

"Which are?"

"I was hoping you'd join me in the garage. I read that book you gave me, and I figured out the adjustments necessary to clear up that funny noise the car makes." Then, whispering in my ear, he added, "And I wanted to show you how happy I am to be back home."

I was back in my sweatshirt in five minutes. So much for the new me, I sighed to myself.

Chapter Ten

After Christmas vacation my relationship with Derek took a dramatic new turn. Well, perhaps dramatic is too strong a word—in truth, the changes at first were so insignificant I hardly noticed them. But when I did, it was almost too late.

It was great having Derek back again. For the first few days after his return, we were together constantly, playing with the new video games his father had given him for Christmas and driving around in his car. It wasn't so much what we did that made the days special: it was that I was with Derek, who always made me feel fine.

But that weekend the first hint of trouble appeared. We were at our special place at the beach, where Derek had driven me after the basketball game.

"Being away from you made me realize just how much I love you," he said.

"I know exactly what you mean." I was still wearing my cheerleader's outfit, and the short skirt was no match for the cool breezes of the ocean. I pulled closer to Derek to keep warm, and he obliged by draping an arm across my shoulders and turning his body to shield me from the wind.

"I can't help but think about what's going to happen after we graduate."

"Derek," I said soothingly, "that's still a year and a half away."

"But I've been thinking. You'll be going off to Europe—"

"If I can get the money," I cut in, "which is debatable. At this point, my fund is down to thirty-eight dollars and sixty-five cents."

"Good."

"Derek!" I cried, a little impatient. "You know how much I've been looking forward to going. How could you say that?"

"I'm sorry," he said, tossing a pebble into the ocean. "I'd just hate for you to be away from me so long. I really missed you over vacation."

"I missed you, too, but I found ways to keep occupied. I mean, you might as well worry about when we go off to college, too," I said flippantly.

"Don't think that hasn't crossed my mind. I'd die if you went off to California or Hawaii or wherever else you've been thinking about."

I gave him a playful laugh, refusing to be

drawn into his serious mood. "What's the matter? Don't you want an educated girlfriend?"

But Derek wasn't laughing. "I mean it, Drea."

"Don't get so bent out of shape," I said. "We're together now, and that's what's important. Besides, I probably won't end up out there anyway. Sam Hennessy says there are lots of good marine biology programs right here in Florida. Who knows? You and I might even end up going to the same school."

Derek wasn't relieved by my words. He threw another stone into the water with all his might. "I may not go to college," he declared. "I'm not cut out for anything."

"Derek, don't be so negative." I twirled my fingers in his hair. "You've got lots of talent."

"Oh, yeah? Like what?"

"Well, you're a good athlete, and there's your photography—"

"I'm not that good," he said.

"Sure you are. And if you'd take my advice, you'd go down to the *Star* and offer to shoot some pictures for them. But that's not all you do. Remember all the times you've helped me straighten out my problems? You've got a pretty analytical mind. I bet you could be an investigator of some sort. Or a lawyer, even."

"I don't know, Drea. I can't decide what I want—not like you."

"You will," I said soothingly. "And I'm willing

to bet that once you decide, you'll give it your best shot and be great at it."

"I don't know—"

"Well, I do," I said, getting slightly exasperated with him. "What's happened to your faith in yourself?"

"I left it in Georgia, I think. I'm sorry, Drea," he apologized. "I brought you out here to kiss, not to hash over the never-ending question of my life. But now I don't feel like it."

"That's OK, Derek. That's what friends are for."

He looked at me and smiled. "You are very special," he said. Then he gave me a little kiss, before helping me to my feet and leading me toward the car.

I wished I could have come up with the answers Derek was searching for, but deep down I knew only he could do that. The one thing I could give him, though, was the emotional support he needed, and I was disappointed he wanted to head back home so soon.

Derek was unusually quiet on the drive home, and I had a feeling there was something on his mind he wasn't sharing with me. Finally, when we were about a block from home, he blurted out, "When were you talking to Sam Hennessy about colleges?"

"Huh?" I had to think for a second, trying to remember the circumstances. "Uh, during vacation. We just got to talking about it."

"Where'd you see him?"

"At the library. He was working on a marvelous report for class."

"Oh," was all he said in reply. Then, trying to sound as casual as possible he added, "Who else did you see while I was away?"

I didn't like the way this conversation was going. "Derek!" I cried. "I didn't *see* anyone. Don't tell me you're jealous!" I was surprised he'd even consider the possibility.

"Me? No," he answered. "I was just curious."

"Yeah, sure," I said uncomfortably. "All I did was talk to another boy. I was not unfaithful."

"I didn't say you were."

"You implied it," I said, feeling hurt at his apparent lack of trust in me.

"I did not!"

I wasn't through. The combination of Derek's reluctance to see me travel and his earlier insecure thoughts made me angry and a little concerned. "What did you do in Georgia, anyway? Did your father put pressure on you? How many girls did *you* go out with?"

"No one!" he cried. "How could you even think—"

"And how could you?" I countered.

"OK. I overreacted, and I apologize," Derek said, the even tone of his voice belying the tension I could see in his body. "It's just that I love you so much I can't help but think the rest of the world feels the same way. I think any guy'd be a fool if he didn't try to steal you away."

"You put me on such a pedestal," I said softly, figuring that Derek's uneasiness with me had to do with some unkind words from his father. "Believe me, no one's beating down my door to ask me out."

"I don't know why not," he said, forcing a smile. "You're very beautiful, Drea."

"Oh, Derek," I said, my anger subsiding. "I'm sorry I yelled at you."

"And I'm sorry I questioned you," he said.

We stared at each other for a moment. "Do you realize we've just had our first fight?" I said with surprise.

"Let's hope it's the last," he said. We were parked in his driveway now, and he moved over to give me a kiss. "I've heard that people should never go to bed angry at each other. Do you forgive me?" he asked.

"Of course," I said, reaching over to stroke his hand. "Let's kiss and make up." Reaching over, I kissed him quickly on his nose.

"Is that the best you can do?" he asked, now smiling.

"I could try again." We kissed again, this time a long and lingering kiss that seemed to go on forever.

"Hmm," Derek murmured after we finally unlocked our hold on each other. "I could get used to fighting if this is what making up is all about."

"Don't you dare," I said, playfully tugging at his chin.

Fortunately, the rest of that weekend Derek was happier and more relaxed. We spent Saturday afternoon watching *Raiders of the Lost Ark* on our VCR, and Derek made the favorable suggestion that we set off on our own archeological hunt. We spent Sunday together, too, watching the football playoffs and just enjoying the wonderful moments of being deeply in love.

Still, despite those romantic two days, that little argument we had had at the beach seemed to open up a sore in our relationship, one that refused to go away over the following weeks. What kept the sore open was a series of circumstances that led me to spend less and less time with Derek.

It was not intentional on my part. With that Monday came the onslaught of school and the first realization that I had other roles besides that of Derek's girlfriend. Mr. Billings made that quite clear. No sooner did we hand in our marine biology reports than he shocked us all by assigning yet another report, due in a month. With no vacation to work in, I prepared myself to give up one night a week to the project until it was done.

I also had my hands full cheerleading at the

basketball games. With the schedule heating up, I found myself at the court two and sometimes three nights a week. Derek would join me for a Coke afterward, but with all the effort I usually gave to cheering on the team, I was all dragged out when it came time for our late-night date. Derek seemed to understand at first, but by the end of January he began to skip the games entirely. He wasn't too pleased, either, with my decision to accept occasional baby-sitting jobs in an effort to build up my Europe fund.

My afternoons, too, were getting busier as a result of my decision to join the school science club. I'd discovered they planned several trips in February and March to some of south Florida's oceanographic institutes, and there was no way I was going to pass up an opportunity like that.

None of this pleased Derek. I wasn't too happy about having to see him less, either, although when I took the time to really think about it, I did have to admit I enjoyed the time we spent apart. It made the time we spent together that much more meaningful, giving me lots more things to talk about than if we'd been with each other the whole time.

But every time I tried to explain that to Derek, he refused to listen. Now that football season was over, he had lots of free time on his hands. He was still down on himself, which in fact *had* been the result of some discouraging remarks by his father, and it was hard to try to continually boost his spirits.

There was only one thing he knew he wanted—me. And he made that more and more clear in ways that began to bother me. One Saturday in early February he asked me go miniature golfing at Castle Park. It was the first time we'd been there in ages, and I was looking forward to going. As I got ready, it occurred to me to invite Natalie and her friend Wendy along. With all I'd been up to lately, I'd been neglecting my little sister, and it seemed the outing would be a perfect way to spend time with two of the people I loved most.

Perhaps I should have asked Derek first, but I honestly thought he wouldn't mind—after all, he'd always treated Natalie like a little sister. And he didn't say anything when he saw the three of us head out to his car, although he did seem a bit tense as he drove down to the big brick castle. It wasn't until Natalie posed to tee off at the first hole—a straightaway through the legs of a lumberjack—that he whispered to me, "Why did you have to bring them along?"

"Why not?" I said.

"I thought we were going to be alone."

"Derek, it's pretty hard to be alone here," I said, looking around. "There've got to be around a hundred people on the course."

"That's not what I mean," he said suggestively.

"There's plenty of time for that later. Besides, did you expect me to cuddle with you on the eighteenth hole or something?"

Not wanting to pursue this any further, I set my ball up on the little green carpet and hit it with all my might. The ball bounced against the lumberjack's foot and dropped a mere six inches from where I'd begun.

Natalie found that terribly amusing. "Even a monkey could do better than that," she teased.

Derek set his ball up on the tee and whispered in my ear, "You still glad you brought her along?"

I was not amused.

We played the next few holes in virtual silence, broken only by the few snide comments Natalie made on my performance. She shut up, however, after I scored a two on a hole that took her six shots to make. Derek was taking it all very seriously, carefully lining up his shots with his club, taking plenty of time before hitting.

"Have you thought about going out for the golf team at school?" I asked after he scored a hole in one.

"It's not the same," he said in a clipped voice.

"Are you still mad I brought Natalie along? They're not bothering us, you know." Natalie and Wendy had spotted a couple of boys on the twelfth hole and were busily speculating on their availability.

It was when we'd reached the fourteenth hole,

the one in which the ball had to loop around a seallike statue posed over a water trap, that I realized what was really bothering him.

"This reminds me," I said. "I'm going to the Sea Institute with the science club on Thursday. I'm going to have to push back our movie date."

"I was looking forward to that," Derek muttered.

I bit my lip. "We can go on Wednesday, can't we?"

"You know, I like the way you go around planning things like I'll go along with anything you say. I'm not your puppy dog." He hit the ball with a loud whack, and no one was surprised when it fell in the water.

"Be quiet," I hissed.

"I won't be quiet!" he yelled. Several people on the next hole turned around to see what was going on, and I felt terribly embarrassed.

Fortunately, Derek knew better than to yell at Natalie. In an act that endeared her to my heart for life, she took Derek aside and told him he was setting a poor example for an impressionable young girl like her. It was enough to calm him down. He came back and apologized.

"I don't know what came over me, Drea. I'm sorry."

"That's OK, Derek," I answered. I wasn't mad at him, but I did want to clear the air.

We got our chance to talk some more a few

hours later after we dropped off Natalie and Wendy at my house. Derek and I retreated to his garage, where wé were insured of privacy.

"OK, why the scene this afternoon? It was so unlike you."

"I don't know," he began.

"Yes, you do. Why can't you tell me?"

He threw up his hands. "We haven't been alone in several days, and then when I pick you up, you had those two little kids with you. You could have told me."

"I didn't think you'd mind," I said. "How many times in the past have we taken Natalie to Castle Park? It's no big deal."

"Maybe to you it isn't. Lately I feel like I'm just another item penciled into your social calendar."

"So you're still upset about that. I'd think you'd want a girl who had other interests in her life."

"But there's hardly any time for me anymore."

"That's not true, Derek. Am I seeing any less of you than during football season?"

He thought about that for a moment. "I don't know."

"Well, I'm not. You're just noticing it more because you've got a lot of free time on your hands. I suggest you do something about it."

"Like what?"

"Did you ever go down to the *Star* and offer to

shoot some pictures for them? Or for the yearbook?"

"No," he said quietly.

"Why not?" I asked, my voice rising.

"Terry Mayhew told me he thought they had all the photographers they needed."

"And you took that as a no?"

Derek nodded.

"Terry's no expert, Derek. Neither am I, but I know enough to see that you shoot better-quality stuff than what's in the paper. Where's that self-confidence you took with you to Georgia, anyway?"

"I don't know, Drea—"

"I'm only going to say this once, Derek. I think you have a lot of talent that could be put to great use in this world. But you're never going to get anywhere if you continue to feel sorry for yourself every time something doesn't go your way. C'mon, Der, you've been through bad visits with your father before, and it's been a month now that you've been depressed. I want you to think real hard about that."

Tiptoeing out the side door, I left Derek to think over the situation he'd put himself in. I hoped he'd shape up fast—I wanted the carefree, easygoing Derek back, the Derek I had fallen in love with.

Chapter Eleven

Valentine's Day came two weeks after that discussion, and I felt it was the perfect opportunity to make things one hundred percent right with Derek and me. Because, believe me, things could have been an awful lot better.

Oh, the movie date that Wednesday night, the one I had to push up a day, went all right. Derek picked out a horror movie with enough scary moments to insure I didn't leave his arms the entire time. He was being extra polite to me—I guess he realized his outburst at the golf course hadn't won him any awards—and at that moment I was as proud and happy to be Derek's girl as I ever was.

Then he had to go ruin it all just two days later. We were on our way to school in his car—ever since he had gotten it, I had abandoned Jane on her morning run—and he handed me a stack of photos he'd shot of me down at the beach.

"Ooh, Derek, these are really good," I told him.

Derek's face moved into a slight grin. "I didn't have anything to do with that. All I did was aim and shoot."

"No, really. These are excellent. I bet you can really do something with this photography. And don't say you can't, 'cause I'm not buying it today."

"OK, I won't say it," he answered.

"When are you going down to the *Star*?"

"You still on that?" he asked, not masking the irritation in his voice. "Forget it. I'm not interested. They're all a bunch of nerds."

I flipped through the photos, determined not to get any further involved in that tender subject on this bright sunny morning. "Say, this is a wonderful shot of the beach. Which reminds me—I found out about the greatest thing at the institute yesterday!"

"What?"

"They're sponsoring a two-month-long study program off the Mexican coast this summer, and they're accepting applications from high-school students for some of the positions. Isn't it exciting?"

"I take it you're applying?"

"Of course I am. Me pass up an opportunity for hands-on experience in the field? Ooh, I hope they accept me."

"I hope they don't." Derek scowled.

"How can you say that?"

"You're talking about the whole summer. What about us?"

"We've got plenty of time," I said. "Can't you see how valuable this could be?"

"What makes you so sure they'll accept you? You don't have any experience with boats or diving. How do you even know you'll like it?"

"I won't know till I try, will I?" I said irritably.

"I'd just as soon you didn't," he replied.

"Say, whose side are you on? Don't you want me to be happy?"

"I want *us* to be happy, and having you go off for the summer isn't going to help. I want you to stay here with me."

"I wouldn't be leaving you," I said. "I *would* be coming back."

"I still don't like the idea," he grumbled.

"It's not for you to decide," I said, annoyed with his attitude. "I don't go around telling you what to do."

"*No?*" Derek shouted. "Try listening to yourself sometime."

For the rest of the ride, I couldn't get another word out of him. Why couldn't he accept and share in my dream? I sank into a shell of my own, hoping we wouldn't end up as one of those couples forever bickering and sniping at each other. Derek had known for years of my desire to travel, and as my friend he never said anything to discourage me from it. But ever since we'd started dating, he'd become so possessive and territorial it was stifling.

Fortunately, Derek was back to his old easy-going self when I called him that night to talk about the Student Follies. Margo had at last rounded up six couples, and we planned to meet the following week for our first rehearsal. We were going to do a song from *Grease*, with costumes and everything.

"I can't wait to hear you sing," I teased him.

"Now wait a second," he challenged. "My shower head thinks I'm the greatest singer in the world. It's your singing I'm concerned about."

"Just you wait," I told him. "I think I can handle it. Besides, it's all in the costumes. When I told Mom about the act, she offered me a choice of some of her old clothes to wear onstage."

"Your mother was a greaser?" he exclaimed.

"Well, not a greaser, but she used to wear her hair in a ponytail and everything."

We must have talked for over an hour, speculating about our parents' past and what it was like to really be a teenager back in the late fifties. We talked about everything but us—and it was one of the best talks we'd had in a long, long time.

So I thought I'd hit on the perfect Valentine's Day gift for him—his own genuine 1950s greaser shirt, which I found after going to various thrift shops.

The card I got to go along with it fit right

with the theme, too. On the front was a cartoon of two greaser types locked in an embrace. (Actually they were closer to New Wave types than greasers, but it was the best I could find.) On the inside it said, "To my rock 'n' roll sweetheart: Happy Valentine's Day." I wrapped it up in bright shiny red paper and stuck a big white bow on top. I couldn't wait until he opened it.

The school was holding a Valentine's Day dance that Saturday night, and by plan we agreed to give each other our gifts right before we left. I had the present in my hands, all ready to give to him, when he came through the front door, but I held back when I saw what was in his hands: one dozen long-stemmed roses.

"Derek, I don't believe this. These must have cost you a fortune!"

"Is that all you're going to say?" He smiled as he handed me the flowers. "Here, Happy Valentine's Day." Along with the roses, he offered a card. "Open it."

Inside was one of those flowery, sentimental-looking cards with a long poem describing the many ways of love. "I'm not much of a poet, but this card seems to say exactly what I think of you," he said.

I gulped at his words, a little embarrassed now over the light nature of my gift. "Here," I said, my voice suddenly small. "I love you, Derek," I added.

Derek quickly tore open the package. "What

is this?" he asked, holding up the purple-and-white bowling shirt.

"Congratulations, you're the first on your block to have your very own own greaser's outfit."

"Thanks," he said, trying to force a smile. "Just what I've always wanted."

"Well," I said, trying to make the most of a bad situation, "at least you won't have to worry about a costume for the follies." I wanted to crawl into the nearest hole and die.

"Um, I think we ought to be going to the dance now," Derek said.

"Almost ready," I said, and went into the kitchen, filled a vase with water, and put the roses in it. I took one last sniff of the flowers before leaving them on the table by the door. "They sure are beautiful," I said.

Derek brightened at that remark. Maybe at the dance I could find a more proper way to express my love for him.

I did. We had a wonderful time at the dance, and on our way back Derek detoured to our favorite little park, where he told me again and again how much he loved me and how I'd made this the best four months of his life.

If only things between us could have remained so special. . . .

Chapter Twelve

Two nights later we went to Margo's house for our first follies rehearsal.

"Where are we going to practice?" I asked her as I took my jacket off and stepped into the small living room.

"Right here. I was waiting for another set of strong hands to arrive so we could move some of this furniture," she said, casting a gaze at Derek, who still stood by the front door. "It's just like Jesse to be late at a time like this."

Already scattered around the room were eight people including Jane and Randy. I was surprised to see Melissa Iversal there, as she'd just split with the boy she'd been dating. Everyone else was part of a couple.

"Good to see you, Melissa," I said to the dark-haired girl. "Who's your partner?"

"I told her it's a surprise," Margo cut in, her chubby hands set firmly on her hips. "He's coming with Jesse—whenever that is," she added impatiently.

For the next few minutes we all helped out, maneuvering the two sofas and assorted tables into the adjacent dining room. "Are you sure your parents don't mind?" Jane wanted to know.

"Not for tonight," Margo answered, wiping her brow. "But after this, we're going to need another place."

"We could meet at my house," I ventured.

"It's not much bigger than this," Derek noted. "I'd offer my house, but I don't think my mom could handle twelve of us at once."

Right before we finished, the doorbell rang, and Margo ushered in the four late arrivals. I had my back to the door and didn't see who Melissa's partner was until Margo led him into the middle of the room.

"Guys, I don't know if you all know Sam Hennessy here. He's agreed to be the twelfth man, and from what I've heard, he can even sing!"

"Welcome aboard," Randy said pleasantly. "We need all the help we can get."

"How do you know?" Jane wondered. "We haven't even started yet."

"I see the company I'm in. Believe me, we need the help."

Randy was joking, of course, but the truth was we were a sorry-sounding lot. Margo handed out copies of the song, "Hopelessly Devoted to

You," and we listened to it on the *Grease* soundtrack, then tried it ourselves.

"We sounded awful," Vicky Loessing said when we'd finished. "Maybe we'd be better off just mouthing the words."

"That's against the rules," Margo answered. "C'mon, let's try again."

We sounded a little better the second time around. Not that Derek or I had anything to do with it—we were both practically tone-deaf. But in looking around the room, I steadied my eyes and ears on Sam and realized Margo was right about his voice. It was deep and rich and definitely on key. I wondered how much singing he'd done before this.

By the time we decided to call it quits for the night, we were on our way to sounding reasonably well. We decided to postpone any serious work on the dancing until we were able to stretch out in a bigger space. It was Sam who finally came to the rescue on that, offering the use of his parents' double garage.

Still, I was surprised when Sam rushed up to me the next day in class. "It sure was great seeing you last night."

I felt like asking why, but didn't. Instead, I just went and took my customary seat by the window. Sam followed me. "I didn't know you were interested in the follies," I said when I realized he had no intention of taking his seat.

"I wasn't, really. But when Teddy broke up

with Melissa, he didn't want to be in it anymore. They needed another guy, and Jesse naturally thought of me."

"Why naturally?"

"He knew I could sing."

"Modest, aren't we?"

"Just honest," he said self-assuredly. "By the way, have you applied for the summer program at the institute?"

"Yes."

"I was hoping you did," he answered. "So did I."

I thought that was peculiar until he added, "Say, you and Derek still a team?"

"Sure," I said. "Couldn't you tell that last night?"

"Not from the way you were looking at me."

"I don't know what you're talking about," I said uncomfortably.

"Sorry, I could have sworn I was being flirted with." He winked before taking his seat two rows behind me.

I don't think I'm exaggerating when I say that Sam had his eyes on me during the entire class. I could *feel* his gaze, even though I didn't once look back to confirm my own suspicions. I didn't think I'd flirted with him the night before. True, I did find myself looking at him every now and then, but no more so than I would at anyone who struck me as being in the wrong place at the wrong time. Still, it bothered me a lot that he'd read more into my gaze than was there. I was in love with Derek, and that was it. Sam had to see that.

The funny thing was, over the following weeks Sam's remarks did cause me to pay him more attention. I wasn't sure why—he wasn't all that good-looking, and besides our interest in biology, we didn't seem to have much in common. But there was no denying it—some indescribably attractive thing was beginning to make him seem very desirable.

I tried to fight it. Every time he entered my thoughts, I had this conversation with myself. It went something like: Drea, how in the world can you have these feelings? Derek is the boy you love, the boy you're committed to. You can't be interested in someone else. It's unfaithful and disloyal.

But as much as I berated myself, there was nothing I could do to stop my heart from pounding furiously whenever Sam was around.

Believe me, I tried. In the weeks that followed, I paid more attention to Derek than I had in a while, switching my schedule around so that I drove home from, as well as to, school with him. Fortunately, basketball season was over, and my cheerleading duties were ending, so I had that extra time to spend with him as well.

All this attention was not lost on Derek, who was much less moody now. At the follies rehearsals, for instance, he was very much at ease, clowning around with the guys and showing off his prowess as a dancer by improvising on the steps that Margo had worked out. At such moments I was so proud of him, proud that the scrawny little boy I'd grown up with had turned into a handsome, outgoing guy who, if he wanted to, could charm any girl he pleased.

But my pride in Derek still couldn't mask this other problem named Sam looming on the horizon. I tried to avoid Sam, in class and at all of the follies rehearsals, but one night at rehearsal, he looked particularly nice, dressed in a tank-top and cutoffs that showed off his lean and slightly muscled legs. My heart caught in my throat when I saw him, and unfortunately, he noticed.

"When are you going to stop fighting it?" Sam whispered to me during one of our breaks.

"What are you talking about?" I turned away from him and focused on Derek, who was engaged in a discussion with Jane, Randy, and Melissa.

"You know very well what I'm talking about, Drea," Sam said. "I know you're interested in me, but you seem just as interested in playing games. What gives?"

"You have an overactive imagination, Sam," I lied. I quickly excused myself and rushed over to Derek, who was babbling some nonsense about our progress on the act.

I glanced at Sam and saw him shake his head

wistfully. Inside I was a jumble of emotions. I couldn't be infatuated with him—I didn't want to be interested in him at all—but it was clear to me that I was.

I felt both mentally and physically drained by the time the night was over.

"I'm exhausted," I said to Derek on the way home from Sam's.

"Maybe I could do something to perk you up," he suggested.

I knew what he meant, but I was definitely not in the mood. "Not tonight, Der. I think what I need now is a hot bath and a good night's sleep."

"I understand," he said.

When he walked me to my door, Derek paused to give me a good-night kiss. I wanted to enjoy it, believe me I did, but it was a kiss like those in the early days of our relationship, when Derek didn't know how. I felt nothing.

I put up a good front, though. "Thanks, I needed that," I told him when our lips parted. "Good night, Derek," I said, hoping he wouldn't see through my lie.

The phone was ringing when I walked in, and I heard my father call, "Drea, is that you?"

"Here, Dad," I said, walking toward the family room where he sat with the phone receiver.

"It's for you," he said. "Jane."

"I'll take it in the kitchen." Then, picking up the extension, I said, "Hey, what's up?"

"That's what I want to know," my friend said. "You were anything but yourself tonight."

"Nothing's up," I said. "I'm just tired, that's all."

"C'mon, Drea, you're not that good an actress. Something's bothering you. Tell me you don't want to talk about it, if you don't, but don't tell me nothing's bothering you. I know better."

"You're right," I said, slumping into a chair. "And I think I need to talk about it very much." In a rush I told her about my bottled-up feelings for Sam and how they were confusing me regarding Derek.

"Gosh, Drea," Jane said when I'd finished. "You mean to tell me you've been carrying all this inside you for over a month? That's enough to drive anyone crazy."

"Thanks for the encouragement."

"I can't say I'm surprised, though. I knew something like this was bound to happen."

"Great, that's all I need, an 'I told you so.' "

"Sorry," Jane said. "I didn't mean it like that. But I think this is your mind's way of saying you're going to have to make a decision one way or another about Derek."

"Like what?"

"Maybe it's time you two let go of the ropes a little."

"You mean break up with him?"

"Or start feeling free to go out with others. Like Sam if you want."

"No," I said emphatically. "I love Derek. I can't leave him."

"I'm not saying you have to. But something's got to give, Drea. You can't go on much longer ignoring Sam. Pretty soon everyone else is going to notice, too."

"Maybe if I continue to ignore him, those feelings I have will go away."

"It's possible," Jane said. "But I have a feeling that whatever it is about Sam that's getting to you wouldn't be there if something wasn't lacking in your relationship with Derek."

"But I love Derek," I insisted.

"Drea," Jane said, using a slightly exasperated tone I didn't like, "it hasn't escaped my attention that you've been complaining about his attitude lately. Things aren't that perfect between you two."

"But they've been a lot better since this follies thing started. It's really made him feel good about himself again. That's what the problem was." I couldn't bring myself to confide in her about the kissing part.

"But if that was the only problem, then Sam wouldn't be in the picture at all."

"He's not in the picture," I insisted.

"All you have to do is give him the word, and he will be," Jane said. "You can't deny you're turning yourself into a nervous wreck over this."

"But I could never hurt Derek," I insisted.

"You may have no choice."

* * *

I tried to convince myself that Jane was wrong, but over the following days two things became apparent. One, Sam was still interested in me. He even tried to ask me out again one afternoon after our Science Club meeting. He didn't press the issue when I turned him down, but even I could tell that my "no" wasn't the no of a girl who was inflexible on the issue.

The other thing was, the magic between Derek and me was disappearing. I found myself less and less interested in being alone with him, which really confused me because I liked being with him in public situations as much as ever.

Something was definitely wrong. What proved it to me was what happened a few days before the Student Follies performance. Derek and I were in front of his TV playing Missile Command. The game was real close, both of us keen on the competition—or so I thought. I had just taken over the lead when, still zapping the fast-descending bombs, I was surprised by a real attack from Derek, who grabbed me from behind and started kissing me.

For the first time in our relationship, I was genuinely repulsed by him. "Derek, stop!" I shouted, pushing him away with all my might.

"Hey, what's wrong?" he asked. He hadn't expected me to act like that at all.

From the sound on the TV, I knew my cities were being destroyed, and for some reason I was more concerned about them than about Derek. "Look what you did," I complained. "I had a triple shot all lined up, and you had to go and ruin it."

"It's only a game," he said softly.

"Oh, I see. When you're out in front, it's important, but when I have a chance of winning, you'll do anything you can to take away my advantage."

"Why are you so angry?" he asked. "Since when do you get angry when I kiss you?" He made a move to approach me again, but for a reason even I was unsure about, I pushed him away.

"There's a time and a place for everything," I said.

"For gosh sakes, Drea, there's no one around now! How could this not be the right time!"

"It was my turn," I insisted.

"Are you going to let a silly game stand between us?" he asked. "What's happened to us, Drea?"

"Nothing's happened," I said.

"But you used to never be able to get enough of me. Now you're turning me away."

"I'm just not in the mood."

"You never seem to be in the mood anymore," he said sullenly.

"That's not true," I shot back. "You're making too much out of this. I'm just not in the mood tonight."

"Then I think you better go now," Derek said abruptly. "I had something more in mind tonight than playing Missile Command."

I didn't want to leave, but a part of me was afraid of what would happen, what I might say, if I pressed on with the conversation. "I think you're right, Der. I'll let myself out. See you tomorrow."

It took me a long time to fall asleep that night. I kept thinking about what my dad had said that time, about not wanting to see either of us hurt. And now for the first time I could see what he meant.

Chapter Thirteen

The next morning things were still tense between us, and on the way to school neither of us said a word. I think we were both hesitant to open the Pandora's box that now lay between us.

That afternoon I came home right after school and made a double batch of brownies. I was feeling so low and confused I could have eaten the entire pan. How could I have ever gotten myself into a situation like this? I wondered.

I thought school would be a refuge from my personal problems, and part of it was exactly that. For the first time I could remember, I longed for first-period PE. Sure enough, the exercises and vigorous basketball game I'd played helped rid me of some of the tension I was carrying around. For that period I was able to concentrate totally on the game and forget that Drea Mallory had anything more important to worry about than how to get a ball down the court.

But reality came crashing down two periods later when I walked into Mr. Billings's marine biology class. Sam was there, and there was no avoiding him. I tried to concentrate on the teacher's lecture and to jump right in when he opened up the class to discussion. But Sam jumped right in with me, and for the rest of the class, we seemed to be the only two participants in the discussion.

I couldn't deny that Sam had some fresh insights to offer; he even managed to stump Mr. Billings on a question or two. Much as I hated to admit it, this was in fact one of the most stimulating classes we'd had. Sam really opened my mind up to new ways of looking at things, and it was a feeling I liked.

I guess I shouldn't have been surprised when he came up to me after class. "You were really something today," he complimented, smiling

"What do you mean?"

"Your comments were right on the mark. I got a lot out of the class because of it."

"If I asked some good questions, it's because you stimulated my thinking," I said truthfully. "It's really exciting when you actually feel you've learned something." I began to make my way out of the classroom, but Sam followed me step for step, and I did nothing to stop him.

"I know what you mean," he said. "Too bad no one else in here seems to think so."

"They don't know what they're missing."

We were in the hallway now, and I held my breath, afraid Derek would run into us. Then I remembered he'd be coming out of gym right then, at the opposite end of the school. Still, I didn't relax. An electricity was flowing between Sam and me, and it kept me from walking away from him. "Where you off to now?" he asked.

"Lunch."

"Well, I have another class," he said. He seemed reluctant to go, and his intense gaze held me in place as well. "Listen, Drea, if you're not doing anything after school, would you like to go to McDonald's with me?"

"You don't give up, do you?" I answered.

"It wouldn't be a date," Sam insisted. "I'd just like to continue our conversation."

"I can't," I said. The truth was, part of me did want to continue our talk, to explore further this *thing* I had for the boy who stood before me. But as long as I was Derek's girl, I knew I couldn't give in to that need. "Maybe some other time, OK?"

Sam smiled broadly at that first hint of a future. "Sure thing," he said. "See ya later."

"Sure," I mumbled, walking away, knowing all the while I had hopes, too, hopes I couldn't put out of my mind. I was going to have to make a decision soon—one way or another.

After lunch—a tuna sandwich I threw away after two bites—I headed to Spanish class, where Derek would be, and took my time getting there. I sat down just as the late bell rang, so there wasn't time to say anything to Derek. But before Mrs. Martinez got things under way, Derek gave me a loving look—his own way, I guess, of reassuring me that everything was going to be all right. I forced a smile back at him, bravely holding back sudden tears, and quickly turned my attention toward the teacher.

Fortunately, I didn't have to see Derek again that day. Baseball practice had begun that week, keeping him after school until four-thirty. They weren't playing games yet—just training to get in shape—so I didn't feel obligated to watch him perform.

Meanwhile, I'd devoured half a pan of brownies thinking about all this, so I decided I'd better get my mind focused on something else. I'll start dinner, I thought, heading toward the refrigerator. Every Tuesday and Thursday since New Year's, when Mom and Mrs. Sebastian had joined the health club, it had become my job to prepare dinner. Sluggishly I took the package of chopped meat out of the refrigerator and began shaping it into a meat loaf. I had it all seasoned and ready for the oven when the back door opened.

"Mom, what are you doing home?"

"Oh, that gym!" she said in an exasperated

tone and threw her purse on the kitchen counter. "They decided to make Thursdays coed night. Of all the nerve!"

"Gee, Mom, I'd think it'd be fun to work out in a room full of gorgeous guys."

"With a body like yours, that's not surprising," Mom said, sitting down at the table. "When you get to be my age, though, you might change your mind."

"You don't have such a bad body," I said.

Mom smiled. "It's nice of you to say. But the only man I'd ever want to face in a leotard is your father. Besides, those gorgeous guys you talked about?" She shook her head. "More like aging men with beer bellies and bald heads."

For some reason the image of my mother in a room full of fat, middle-aged men who were exercising struck me as funny. "Thanks, Mom," I said. "I needed a good laugh."

She took on her concerned-mother look. "Something wrong?"

"Everything."

"That's definitive."

I sat down at the table across from her. "Mom, is it possible to be in love with two boys at the same time?"

Her eyes betrayed her shock at my question. "I suppose it's possible, dear," she began. "But love is a very complicated emotion. It's not as easy to truly love someone as you might think." She looked at me pointedly. "Are you?"

"I don't know," I began, needing to sort out my feelings with someone. "Could we talk about it?"

"Sure, Drea. I had a feeling something was bothering you lately, but I decided not to get involved until you asked."

Nervously I played with my fingers, reluctant to go on, yet needing to voice my confusion. Finally I blurted out, "There's this boy. His name is Sam, and he's in my marine biology class. He's also in the follies with me. I don't know, Mom. I don't understand, but there's something about him I find attractive."

"Attraction doesn't necessarily mean love," Mom pointed out.

"Maybe I shouldn't have used the word love. I mean, I know I'm not in love with him. But I can't stop thinking about him. And then there's Derek."

"And you love him?" she asked cautiously.

"Mom, how can you even question that? I've always loved Derek. You know that."

"There's a difference between the love that two friends can have and the love that belongs to two people who share an emotional commitment. Don't you know that?"

"Sure, Mom, and until Sam was around, I thought Derek and I had that deeper kind of love."

"And now?"

"Now I don't know. Sometimes I don't feel as

strongly toward Derek as I have in the past. I want to, but I don't."

"You can't force love, Drea," Mom said softly. "It's either there or it isn't." She paused but looked like she wasn't done speaking. "Drea, have you felt any pressure from me to hang onto Derek?"

"Derek and I both know how pleased you and Mrs. Sebastian are with our dating. And in a way, I suppose I do feel like I'm letting you down, Mom."

"If that's all that's standing between you and this Sam, then forget it. Marcia and I are both mature women. We'd never force you into anything you didn't want."

"I don't know what I want!" I cried. "I mean, I know I can't cope with the way things are now, but I have just as hard a time coping with the prospect of breaking up with Derek."

"Maybe you could date Derek and Sam."

"Only in some make-believe world, Mom. You may not know it, but Derek has a terrible jealous streak. He wouldn't stand for sharing me with anyone. And to tell you the truth, I don't know if I could take sharing him with another girl, either."

"How have you been getting along?"

"What do you mean?"

"If Sam wasn't around would your feelings for Derek be any different?"

"It's funny. Most of the time I don't know of

anyone else I'd rather do things with. But those times when we're—" I hesitated.

"Alone?" Mom filled in for me.

"Yes," I said softly, reluctant to share this part of my relationship with my mother. "I used to love being alone with him, but now . . . I just don't feel that way."

Mom thought for a moment. "Have you ever considered that you and Derek were meant only to be friends? I think I see now what your father's been worried about all this time. You've been the best of friends for many years now. It would be a shame to see you lose that."

"I don't want to lose it." I could feel tears beginning to well up in my eyes. "Mom, why does it have to be this way?"

Mom reached over and took my hand. "I wish it didn't," she said, trying to mask the tears rising in her own eyes. "But you may have to risk losing that friendship for good in order to keep it."

"I don't understand. How could I do that?"

"Think about this, Drea. What's going to happen to your friendship if things continue the way they are now?"

"I don't know."

"Well, what if Derek becomes angry and frustrated when he realizes your interest in him has waned. Think about how that might lead to arguments and fights and more hurt feelings.

Think about what kind of friendship you'll end up with if that happens."

"But what kind of friendship will we have if I tell him I don't want to see him anymore? I don't want to lose him as a friend, Mom. I'd die if that happened. Oh, why can't we go back to the way it used to be before we started dating."

"You can't turn back the clock, dear. But you can go on from where you are now and build a new level of friendship."

"Do you really think that's possible?"

"I can't predict how Derek is going to act, but knowing him as I do, if you decide to break up with him, he's probably not going to take it lightly. He may act like he's fine, but inside he'll be hurting a lot. He may even decide he doesn't want to be friends with you anymore."

"Mom, what am I going to do?" I wailed, unable to stop the tears from falling now.

Mom got up and put her arms on my shoulders. "Mothers don't always have the answers. You've always had good instincts, Drea. You'll do what you know is right. Both Dad and I will be here to help you along, but in the end it's all up to you."

"It would have been an awful lot easier if I had never gone out with him."

"Don't dismiss the past six months of your life just like that, Drea. It hasn't been all bad, has it?"

I turned around, my eyes glossed over with

tears. "Thanks, Mom. You're right. Only it doesn't make my decision any easier."

"I know, dear," Mom said, hugging me.

The tears came pouring out now in a torrent. Mom, no longer fighting her own tears, held me in her arms and rocked me gently, the way she did when I was a little kid. But I wasn't a kid anymore. I was sixteen and a half years old—and about to make the most important decision of my life.

Chapter Fourteen

In the next two days I learned what a big difference there was between deciding to do something and actually doing it.

That night at dinner I was especially grateful for the TV news, the sound of which drowned out any possibility of conversation—for once in my life I didn't feel like talking to anyone. Or eating, for that matter. I barely picked at my food, my hamburger tasting like dog food to me. Only Mom seemed to notice, and I knew she understood there were some things in life more important than dinner.

After our conversation I had just about convinced myself that I had to make the move and break up with Derek. The choice seemed clear-cut—either break up with him now and use the good feelings we still had for each other to build a new, platonic friendship, or continue with the way things were and let the relationship deteriorate until we ended up enemies.

But when I went to my room after dinner to think, the choices blurred together. Either choice, it seemed, led to the unalterable conclusion that Derek and I would never date again. And as much as my brain told me that was what had to be, the signal still hadn't reached my heart. Derek was too much a part of my life to simply drop.

If I needed any more proof, all I had to do was look around my room. Everywhere I looked, there was something to remind me of him. The program from the first Dolphins game we went to together, the tiny stuffed whale he bought me after our fight at the beach, the Valentine's Day card still taped to my mirror, even my old Little League baseball cap. So much of my entire life was intertwined with this boy I had grown up with. How could I just simply cut the ties?

I let myself give into the tears again and for the longest time cried my heart out for what I knew I had to do. I cried for the countless times I'd poured out my troubles to Derek and for the way he'd always listen and do his best to ease my suffering. I cried for the times we'd sit alone, just the two of us, and talk about nothing in particular and think it was the greatest time in the world. I cried for the times Derek took me in his arms and told me he loved me and how it made me feel so complete and so perfect. I cried for the times I fantasized about how wonderful it would be to be Mrs. Derek Sebastian someday. I cried for the realization that growing up means that not all your dreams can come true and that somehow you just have to accept that and go on with the rest of your life.

Before I went to sleep that night, I told myself I'd break up with Derek the next day. Better to get it over with now, I figured, than to let it drag on any longer.

But when I saw him the next morning, my resolve weakened. Derek was in an unusually exuberant mood, brought on by his pleasure with yesterday's baseball practice and his excitement over the upcoming follies.

"Randy and Adam were over last night, and they loved the shirt you got me," he said breezily on our way to school. "They said I'll be the most authentic-looking greaser in the bunch."

"I'm glad," I said weakly, looking out my window at the passing scenery.

"Boy, I can't wait till dress rehearsal tonight. Should be lots of fun," he continued.

"Yeah."

"Drea, something wrong?" he asked.

"No," I answered, forcing a smile. "It's just that time of the month, you know?" I hated myself for coming up with such a lame excuse, but I couldn't seem to muster the courage to tell him the truth at this point.

"I hope you'll be all right for tonight. It's going to be so much fun, I'd hate for anything to spoil it for you."

The love and concern in his voice nearly made me cry all over again. Why did he have to be such a caring person? Why couldn't he be an egotistical bore like Roger and make it easy for me to say what I had to say? I could barely look at him, realizing that if I did, I'd lose all my nerve for sure.

Derek took his right hand off the stick shift and brushed my shoulder. "Feel better," he said. "I love you."

That did it. The remnants of my resolve to break up with him disappeared entirely; there was just no way I could force the words out now. "Thanks, Derek," I answered him. "I'm sure I'll be up for tonight."

I gave it my best shot, that's for sure. The dress rehearsal took place in the auditorium, and the festive atmosphere temporarily helped take my mind off the situation. That plus the exaggerated makeup that everyone in our group wore made Derek and Sam look so unlike themselves that I could pretend they were different people altogether.

The dress rehearsal was a run-through of the entire program, and so we waited in the dressing rooms for our act to be called. Since we were the third to the last act in the entire show, it was a very long wait. I spent most of the time just wandering among the crowd, chatting aimlessly with my friends and stopping to watch some of them perform. It was easier for me to play social butterfly than to force myself to make conversation with Derek. Every time he was near and I thought about what I had to do, the butterflies in my stomach fluttered furiously, truly making me nauseous.

Derek seemed to be doing all right for himself. Every time I spotted him he was involved in conversation. His dark red hair, even slicked down, was recognizable, although his outfit and makeup did make him look like John Travolta's younger brother. At one point he and a few of the guys—Sam included, I noticed with a shock—were locked arm in arm, strutting across the room like a bunch of wild chorus boys and laughing hysterically. It was a funny sight, and despite myself I laughed, too, although it was hardly enough to make a dent in my depression.

Then, shortly before we were due to go on, I noticed Derek in an animated discussion with Melissa. I had no idea what they were talking about, but whatever it was, it was making Derek smile. For the first time in several days, I felt the weight on my heart slowly begin to rise. I was glad Derek was enjoying this conversation with another girl. Not too long ago, that thought would have sent me into a tailspin of jealousy, but now it pleased me to no end. This must mean I am ready to let him go, I told myself. Let him go to find another girl just like I will find another boy.

So the time had come. Or almost, I should say. I'd decided then to break the news to Derek the following night—right after the follies. There was no reason to ruin this event for both of us, I reasoned. Let our memory of the follies be a happy one, one we could always look back on fondly as the last thing we did together as a couple.

With that decision firm in my mind, I walked over to Derek and the rest of the group. Putting on my best smile, I took his hand and followed him onto the stage.

"Feeling up for it?" Derek whispered as we got into position.

"Sure," I answered bravely. "I'm the original trouper, remember?"

The curtain rose, and for the next five minutes I lost myself in the character of a 1950s teen, one who didn't have a care in the world and for whom life was just a continuous series of happy events. If only *my* life could be like that, I thought fleetingly, as I sang, "hopelessly devoted" to my love.

Strangely enough, the tension I felt over Derek helped make my performance onstage easier. I pretended the words were coming out of someone else's mouth, and the dance steps from someone else's feet. I even managed to crack a smile at one point as Derek twirled me in his arms in time with the rest of our troupe. We must have done all right, for our shuffle off the stage was greeted with warm applause from the stagehands, not to mention a few wolf whistles as Margo flashed her poodle skirt over her knees.

"Congratulations, gang! We did it!" Margo shouted when we were back in the dressing room.

"Now if we can only do it again tomorrow night," Jane said.

"Where's your confidence, girl?" Margo chided. "We're gonna be even better tomorrow, right?"

"Right!" we all responded, though I wondered how in the world I'd ever be able to make it through another performance.

"Who's up for going to the Center?" Randy asked.

"Like this?" Melissa cried. "I didn't bring a change of clothes."

"Who did?" Randy answered, looking every bit the greaser with his slick black hair and leather jacket. "Let's go as we are. Whaddya say?"

Melissa shrugged and joined the small crowd that was making its way toward the exit.

"Coming, Drea?" Derek asked me.

"I'm not feeling so hot," I answered. "Cramps, remember?"

"I understand," he said. "I'll drive you home, then."

"No, you go on with the others. I'll bum a ride off someone here."

"I can't let you do that. C'mon, let me take you home."

"Derek," I said, putting some emphasis in my voice, "I don't want to spoil your fun. Go on now with the others."

"Are you sure, Drea? This isn't like you at all."

"I'll be all right," I said. "I already spoke to Lynn Quincy, who said she would take me home. Now go before I physically kick you out." I tried to keep my tone light but insistent. I knew I couldn't bear to ride with Derek under any conditions, and a glance at Sam, who stood by the door with Jesse and Margo, convinced me the Center was the last place I wanted to be.

"Well, OK," he said at last. "If you insist. I'll call you later." He bent over to kiss me goodbye before walking out.

"Goodbye, Derek," I said quietly after he was gone. "Goodbye."

Chapter Fifteen

I was sitting in the kitchen the following morning, finishing up my breakfast of tea and toast when the doorbell rang. Natalie ran to get it, and seconds later came into the kitchen to get me. But before she could say a word, Derek came marching through the kitchen door.

"Morning, Drea," he said apologetically. "Sorry to bother you so early, but I had to find out how you were. I've been worried since last night. Your mom said you'd gone to bed when I called."

Instinctively I pulled my terry robe tightly across my chest. "I guess I was a bit abrupt last night," I said, trying to sound as casual as possible.

"What happened?" Natalie took the seat next to me and leaned forward expectantly.

"None of your business," I said to her. "Derek, why don't you go to the family room while I put on some clothes? I'll be just a minute." Brushing past him in a rush, I made my way to my room and threw on a pair of cutoffs and a top, the first things I could find.

When I got to the family room, Derek was already sitting in Dad's chair. "So, how was the Center?" I asked in as casual a tone as I could muster under the circumstances.

"It wasn't the same without you," Derek said. "I was really concerned. You were pretty agitated last night."

"You mean you didn't have a good time?" Somehow I thought since I wasn't there, Derek might have opened up to some of the other girls in the group. But seeing him look at me now with obvious concern made me realize how wishful that thinking had been.

"I couldn't stop thinking about you. It was just so unlike you to act that way."

Suddenly I realized I couldn't wait until that night to break up with Derek. I had to do it right then, for the simple reason that I didn't want to lie to him anymore. "Derek, it *was* unlike me. I haven't been myself lately."

"I know. You said—"

"I fibbed about not feeling well," I told him, taking my customary prone position on the sofa. "You of all people should have seen through that. You know those things have never bothered me before."

"I had no reason not to believe you," he said. "But why did you find it necessary to lie?"

"Because it was easier than telling you the truth."

"I don't understand. What are you driving at?"

"The truth was I didn't want to party with you last night. You see, lately something's come over me. This feeling. I don't really know how to explain it. It has to do with us . . . with the way I feel about you."

Derek raised his hand to his brow in a thoughtful gesture. "You're right, you're not making sense."

I wasn't sure what to say next. It was more difficult than I had expected. "Let me see if I can put it another way. Do you remember the last time you kissed me?"

"Sure. Last night. Before I left."

"Do you remember what it felt like?"

"It felt like it always does."

"Which is?"

"Oh, I don't know. Nice. Loving. It's kind of hard to put into words. . . ."

"Well, Derek, I don't know how to say this to you, but I didn't feel the same thing. Oh, it felt nice, but there was a time once when just the thought of your kissing me made me tingle all over with excitement."

"Maybe I need more practice," he said lightly.

I lifted my head up and faced him head on, tears now brimming in my eyes. "You don't understand. I've lost that, Derek. I've lost it, and I don't think it's ever coming back." I couldn't say any more as I was overcome with tears. I bent over, my head in my lap, and let myself cry.

"Drea. Drea." Derek leaned over and rubbed the back of my neck. "Don't cry. Please don't cry." I could hear his own voice getting hoarse. "We can work it out, you'll see."

"*You* don't see," I said through the sobs. "It's not going to work, Derek. It's gone beyond that. I—I don't think we should date each other anymore."

"Don't say that, Drea," Derek pleaded, fighting back his own tears. "You don't mean it!"

I shook my head. "I do. I wish I didn't, but I do."

"No, Drea. I don't believe it. It's a joke. Your idea of an early April Fool's gag, right?"

My only response was to shake my head no.

Derek came over to the sofa and took me in his arms. We were both crying heavily now, as if the tears could miraculously purge us from the hurt we were each carrying inside. It was strange. In all the years I'd known Derek, I'd seen him upset, but I'd never seen him cry. It hurt me terribly to be the one to cause him so much pain. But for Derek's sake I knew I had to be strong and not back away from my decision. In a way I felt relieved to have finally told him, but I knew I was still a long way away from letting him down as easily as I could. I let him cry after my own tears were spent, comforting him like the friend I considered myself to be, until at last his tears were gone.

But even then, I continued to hold on to him, for just a little while longer, in this brief moment we'd opened our souls to each other. I felt closer to him then than I had ever felt to anyone else in the world. It seemed so crazy that I had to break up with Derek to experience this closeness. I only hoped that he could feel it too and understand it as something far more important than my just being his girlfriend.

But Derek pulled back and retreated to the chair. He refused to look at me, focusing his attention on the assorted mess on the coffee table. "I thought you loved me," he said sullenly.

"I do love you. I still do," I insisted. "I don't want to jeopardize that love. That's why I think we have to break up now."

"That doesn't make any sense, Drea."

"But it does," I told him. "I've loved you, Derek, ever since you were a shy, lonely little boy on a Little League bench, aching for a friend to confide in. I've loved you through all the years I've dated other boys and you were around to pick up the pieces afterward. I've loved the times we've spent together as friends and consider those times the most precious part of my life. I thought that by dating you it would make that friendship much more complete—and for a while it did. But somewhere along the line I discovered that being your girfriend wasn't the way to go."

"I thought we had some pretty good times—"

"We did, Derek, some of the best times I've ever had. I'm grateful for them. But we've had some not-so-good times, too. Fights, even. I can't ever remember having a fight with my *friend* Derek. But I seemed to get into several of them with my boyfriend Derek."

"But all couples fight."

"Does that make it right?" I challenged. "I thought a long, long time about this before telling you. And I kept coming to the same conclusion—if I continue to be your girlfriend, I'll lose the opportunity of remaining your friend. And, Derek, I'd much rather be your friend for the rest of our lives than be your girlfriend for another few months and then never see you again. Now, given that choice, which would you rather have?"

"But why does there have to be a choice? I mean, why can't we go on as we are?" he pleaded.

"I wish it could, but I can't will my body to feel something it doesn't feel any more."

"Maybe you'll change."

"Who knows? Maybe in a month I'll regret having made this decision. But it's not fair to either one of us to hold on, hoping for a miracle. You deserve someone who really wants you, not someone who's living on past memories."

"I don't know how I'll make it without you."

"You will. But believe me, it's not going to be easy for me, either. The important thing is we'll still have our friendship. I'm not walking out on your entire life, remember." I tried to raise a smile. "I'm still your next-door neighbor, and you're not getting away so easily. I'll always be here to talk. You can count on that."

"Was it something I did? Something I said? I could change, you know."

"I don't want you to change. You're a wonderful boy, Derek. Correction—young man. You're handsome, clever, funny, and you even have a car. I bet the girls will be lining up down the block for a date, once word gets around that you're free."

"I don't want anyone else, Drea," he insisted.

"You will, you'll see. I know it. Gosh, Derek, I'm the only girl you've ever gone out with. Aren't you even just a little bit curious about what it'd be like with someone else?"

"Do you have someone else?"

"It doesn't make any difference," I said, thinking that now wasn't the time to bring up Sam. "Whether I do or not, I still think we're making the right decision."

"What about tonight?" he asked suddenly. "You don't really expect me to go through with that act now."

"I'd planned to tell you after the show, but in a way I think it's better this way. Let's see if we can get through it together—as friends. It's going to be hard for me, too. What do you say, partner?" I smiled weakly.

"You don't leave me much choice." Derek forced himself to smile, too. "I'll try," he said.

I'll say this much for Derek, he did a lot more than try. He put up a brave front for everyone in the group, kidding around with the boys as usual, not turning away when Margo or Melissa or Jane wanted a word with him. If he appeared to be a little distant to me, no one noticed. In fact, the only one who even knew about us was Jane, and that was simply because I asked her for a ride to the school. Even then, she knew only of the decision—I hadn't the strength to go into the details with her; and Jane, being the good friend that she is, knew it was too soon for me to talk.

And no one seemed to pay much attention when both Derek and I decided not to attend the little party Margo had at her house after the follies. Partying was the farthest thing from my mind. That night, the first Saturday night in a long, long time, I stayed home.

Chapter Sixteen

Bleary-eyed from a sleepless night, I stumbled into the kitchen the following morning. Dad was already hovering over the stove like a short-order cook, whipping up a batch of blueberry pancakes, and Mom was buried in the newspaper as usual. Natalie glared at me as soon as I walked through the door.

"Morning, sleepyhead," Dad said pleasantly. "Pancakes?"

"Sure, Dad." I may have been feeling low, but that didn't stop me from being hungry. I made myself a cup of tea and joined the others at the table.

"I didn't hear you come in last night," Mom said, putting down the paper.

"I think I got back before you did," I answered. "I caught a ride with Lynn Quincy right after the show, then went right to bed. Say, what'd you think of the act?"

"You were wonderful," Mom said, beaming. "And Derek—" She stopped awkwardly, probably thinking I didn't want to be reminded of him.

"Yeah, Mom, Derek was pretty good, too, wasn't he?" I said, trying to sound cheerful.

Dad smiled. "Andy, you looked just like your mother in that outfit. Sure brought back a lot of memories."

"And the audience loved you," Mom said. "You were the hit of the show."

"Ah, we were just out to have fun," I said, taking another sip of my tea.

At this point we would have expected Natalie to add her two cents' worth—after all, she'd gone to the show with my parents, and she was never at a loss for words. But she was unusually silent, placing all her attention on mopping up the maple syrup on her plate.

"Tell Drea what you thought of her, Natty," Mom urged.

"I think Drea stinks," she spat out.

"Natalie!" three voices shouted.

"You're mean and awful and heartless. I hate you!" she went on, her voice rising with emotion.

"What'd I do?" I asked, baffled.

"You know what you did. You dumped Derek, and I hate you for it!"

"Natalie—" Dad said, a warning tone in his voice.

"No, Dad, let her go on," I said. I'd told Natalie the news after Derek had left, as I knew her curiosity had been aroused by the crying she'd heard from the family room. She had seemed to take it all in stride, not commenting to me one way or the other about it—until now. "It really bothers you, doesn't it?" I said gently.

"How could you be so mean?" she wanted to know. "Derek never did anything to hurt you."

"That's true," I said. "And if there was a way I could have done it without hurting Derek, I would have. I didn't want to, Natalie. It's just that sometimes relationships don't work out the way you want them to. Like you and Jonathan Cooper. Remember when you used to get all excited and happy whenever he talked to you? And remember how thrilled you were when he finally asked you to a dance and how much fun you had? And then how after a while the thrill disappeared until you weren't interested in him anymore?"

"That was different. Jonathan's a creep," she said.

"You didn't used to think so. That's because you changed your mind as you got to know him better. Well, something like that happened with Derek and me."

"But Derek's not a creep."

"I still like Derek very much, Natalie. But as I got to know him a lot better, I realized that I didn't love him the way a girl should love a boyfriend. It hurts me to realize I feel that way, but I do, and there's nothing I can do to change it. I'd only hurt Derek even more if I hid the way I felt. Do you understand what I'm saying?"

"Sort of," she admitted. "But if you're breaking up with him, that means I'm never going to see him anymore, either."

"Is that what's really bothering you?" I asked, breaking into a slight smile. "Derek and I are still friends. And he's still your friend too, silly. Besides, next-door neighbors don't disappear so easily."

"Well," she began, "all I've got to say is you'd better be right." She was about to reach into the platter for some more pancakes when the doorbell rang. Putting her fork down, she said, "I'll get it," and raced to the front of the house.

As soon as she was out of earshot Dad said, "I'm proud of you, Andy. I think you made a very mature decision."

"It wasn't easy," I said.

"Part of what makes us grow wiser is the ability to make the hard decisions," he continued. But the rest of what he had to say was cut off as Natalie led Derek into the kitchen. All of us turned to face him, Mom and Dad even looking a bit awkward and no one able to say a word.

"Derek, what are you doing here?" I finally asked, pulling away from the table.

"Can I talk to you for a minute?"

"OK," I said tentatively, rising from my seat. I

led Derek out of the kitchen and into the living room. "What can I do for you?" I said, trying to keep my tone light.

He shuffled around a little before speaking up. "Well, actually, what I had in mind was . . . well, the Yankees are playing the Dodgers today, and I thought it'd be fun to go see them. I was, um, wondering if you'd be interested in coming along."

"Oh, Derek, you know I can't."

"It's not a date or anything. You know, just two friends out to enjoy the game."

I felt a jumble of emotions vying for attention inside me. I truly would have enjoyed going, but I knew now was the wrong time. As much as Derek would pretend it was a "friendly outing," it really would be a date, and I didn't want to encourage him. "No, Derek," I repeated. "I'm not interested."

"But you love baseball—"

"That's not the point. I told you yesterday, we as a couple aren't going to work out. It's not a good idea for us to do anything together right now. I'm sorry."

"I see," he said, suddenly growing colder. "You've got better things to do than waste your time with me."

"Derek, don't do this to yourself—or me," I pleaded. "You don't know how hard it is for me to refuse you like this."

"So don't."

"Derek, we went over all this yesterday. I don't think we should date anymore. Please don't make it any harder on either of us than it has to be."

"You haven't exactly made it easy on me."

"Please, Derek, try to understand."

"But if it's so hard for you, too, why are you doing this?"

"Because I can see what's down the road for us if we don't. I told you, Derek, more than anything I want to remain friends with you. Please don't ask for anything more than that. I can't give it to you."

"Drea—" I could see the tears forming in Derek's eyes, and I couldn't bear to see him cry again. Turning away, I said flatly, "Please go home, Derek. Now."

The door slammed shut behind me, and for a few seconds I stood in place numbly. Mom came out, then, to see what was going on, and as soon as I made eye contact with her, I let loose with a torrent of tears. Mom took me in her arms and let me cry for what seemed like forever.

Chapter Seventeen

For the next few weeks Derek did his best to avoid me.

That Monday morning, for instance, he left for school much earlier than usual just so he wouldn't have to see me leave my house. In Spanish class he barely acknowledged my presence. And to avoid any further awkward moments, I returned to my original seat on the other side of the room. Around the neighborhood it was as if he'd moved a thousand miles away—he never was around. I knew, because I hardly ever saw his car in the garage.

I figured Derek was still angry and hurt, but this total rejection of me was something I hadn't counted on. Although I couldn't let it interfere with my decision, the truth was, I really missed his friendship. Maybe it was foolish of me to have thought we could go on as just friends, to think I could ask him to turn off the sweetheart stuff and just be nice to me. Maybe it was a stupid, selfish wish on my part that didn't make sense in the real world.

It didn't take long for word of our breakup to filter among the rest of the junior class. I found out soon enough that very Monday in marine biology. Sam, trying to sound very concerned, told me he'd heard the news and wanted to know if this now meant I could accept a date from him. I told him it did and made a date with him for that Friday night. For some reason, though, I wasn't as excited about the prospect as I was when it was something I fantasized about. But I still felt it would be good to get back into circulation and see what being with another boy was like after all these months.

Unfortunately, the date was a disaster. For starters, I was a bit put off by the way he took charge and told me we were going to a concert that night. Derek and I always talked about our options and made decisions together, or if Derek had something particular in mind, he'd *ask* me first if I was interested or not. But Sam seemed to take for granted that anything he'd want to do I'd want to do—and that, I found, was a mistake.

The concert Sam took me to was a *symphony* concert, of all things. My jaw nearly dropped to the floor when he told me, on our way to the auditorium.

"I thought you meant the Foreigner concert," I said, unwilling to hide my disappointment. The rock group was playing in Fort Lauderdale that night, and that was the only concert anyone in school was talking about.

"I never told you that. Rock music bores me," he added disdainfully. "I thought you were a real music lover."

"The symphony's fine," I said, although I really wasn't sure. The last time I'd gone to a classical music concert was when I was about seven and Mrs. Sebastian and my mom dragged Derek and me into Miami, to expose us to some culture. "I just wish I'd known. I feel terribly underdressed." Somehow I had a feeling that my skin-tight jeans and camisole top would not fit in with the symphony crowd, especially since Sam was dressed in a real shirt and a nice pair of pants.

"Don't worry. No one will notice."

Maybe no one noticed, but I *did* feel uncomfortable. The audience was composed mostly of blue-haired ladies from a nearby retirement village. Only a handful of people our age were there.

The music didn't lift my spirits, either. I really had to concentrate to stay awake for the entire performance.

But to hear Sam talk, you would have thought we'd just have stepped out of heaven or something. He thought the orchestra was magnificent, and on the ride back to Seminole Grove, he went on and on about it until I had to practically beg him to stop."

"That's OK," he said when I suggested a change of topic. "I was going to tell you . . . I heard from the institute today. The arrangements for the tour are all set."

"You mean you're in?" I said with surprise.

"Didn't I tell you?" he said with as much puzzlement. "I found out last week."

"Congratulations," I said, feeling disappointment rise from the pit of my stomach. If Sam already had found out he was accepted, the chance of my hearing the same good news now was slim.

"Weren't you accepted?" he asked.

"I guess not. I would have heard by now if I was."

"Too bad," he said, too casually for my hurt ego to bear. "Shame you won't be there. It's gonna be a great trip."

"Yeah," I agreed, focusing my eyes out the window and thinking: Do you have to rub it in?

But Sam didn't notice—or for that matter didn't seem to care—about my disappointment. For the rest of the ride to my house, he speculated about the grand times he'd have this summer. I couldn't believe his insensitivity. Was this the boy I was dying to get my hands on?

Kissing him now was the farthest thing from my mind.

I was relieved when he dropped me off. "Thanks for the date," I said, quickly opening my side of the car. When he started to open his door to walk me to the house, I added, "You don't have to do that," and hurried up the path to the front door.

Thank goodness I still had a sense of humor. Once inside I couldn't help laughing at the absurdity of it. Sam was anything but the boy I'd thought he was, and here I'd spent all this time building him into a demigod. It just goes to show what your mind can do to you.

But the next thought that hit me was: I wish I could tell Derek about this. In the past I always went over my less-than-successful dating ventures with him. And Derek had always managed to find the humor in even the worst situation, sometimes even leaving me laughing so hard it hurt.

But as soon as I thought about it, I knew I'd never tell him. It was only a week since we had broken up, a week in which he'd hardly said two words to me. I knew he wasn't ready to hear about any of my new adventures, especially one involving Sam, whom he'd suspected of stealing my heart a long time ago. No, I'd have to be patient and wait until Derek was ready to accept me back as his friend. I hoped it would happen soon.

In the weeks that followed, my life slowly adjusted to Derek's absence. I concentrated a little harder on my schoolwork and got ready for the upcoming SATs. I took on more baby-sitting jobs around the neighborhood and watched my savings inch up a little closer toward my goal. I got back in touch with girlfriends who somehow always seemed to be crowded out whenever a boy stepped into the picture. But in all that time I never once stopped thinking about Derek.

From what I could tell, he seemed to be getting by all right. Three weeks after we broke up, he won the first game he pitched—a four-hit shutout. He finally took my advice and joined the *Star*'s photography staff, but still he didn't seem interested in any other girls. From what I heard from Randy, Derek spent all his free time hanging out with the boys.

On the day Derek was pitching his second game, I decided to watch. I really did enjoy watching him perform, and even though he still wasn't talking to me, I believed that Derek would appreciate my interest. The game was being played on the field at the far corner of our high school's athletic complex. The stands were small, as very few people went to the games, so Derek was sure to see me watching him at some point.

I took my place on the top row and scoured the approaching ballplayers until I spotted Derek. He was taking his position on the pitcher's mound. As soon as he started pitching, I could tell he was in good form. I could tell because his pitches were curving over the plate just so. If he could keep it up, he was bound to win the game.

I was concentrating so much on Derek that I didn't notice the arrival of a petite, dark-haired girl on the level below me—that is, until I heard her say, "Drea, can you hear me?"

"What?" I mumbled, searching for the body that belonged to the voice. "Oh, hi, Melissa." I smiled. "Haven't seen you in a while. What brings you here?"

"I'm a fan," she said simply. "You?"

"Me, too. Come join me up here."

"Thanks," she said, rising.

"Been to many games?" I asked. "I don't remember seeing you around these parts before."

"This is my first," she admitted, blushing slightly. "I'm a new fan, you could say."

"Hmm, would you care to be filled in on some of the qualities of our team?"

Melissa listened with interest as I pointed out our team's strengths and weaknesses, ending with, "And last but not least, our starting pitcher, Derek Sebastian. Specialty: fastball that sinks to the right when he's on. Has excellent control and a good move to first."

"I'm impressed," Melissa said. Then she added quietly, "About you and Derek, I was really sorry to hear—"

"We're still friends," I cut in quickly.

Melissa said nothing more, focusing her attention on the field. Was it my imagination, or was she, too, hanging on every pitch Derek threw, holding her breath when he made his windup and releasing it only after the ball reached the plate?

"He's really remarkable," she said after Derek struck out two batters in a row in the second inning.

"He sure is," I put in. "But he worked really hard to make himself into a pitcher. When he was eight, they nearly kicked him out of Little League 'cause he was so bad."

"I can't imagine that," she said.

"It's true," I said. I found myself telling Melissa about Derek's infamous Little League career and, in doing so, discovered a pleasant feeling come over me. The Derek I was talking about wasn't the boy I'd just broken up with. This was the Derek I'd always loved, the boy who was my closest and dearest friend. I liked that feeling and promised myself I'd do whatever I could to see if he was ready to think of me in that way, too.

"You really like Derek, don't you?" I asked Melissa.

"Well . . ." she stammered.

"It's OK," I told her. "He's not mine anymore."

"Sometimes I don't think he'll ever be interested in anyone but you."

"Give him time," I said. "I couldn't think of anyone I'd rather see him go out with than you."

"You really mean that?"

I did—and I felt good about saying so. "I'll see if I can put in a good word on your behalf," I said. "But be patient. Derek can be pretty stubborn about these things."

Derek won the game easily, 5–1. Afterward I ran up to congratulate him.

"Drea, what are you doing here?"

"Didn't you see me in the stands? I watched the whole game."

"You didn't have to do that," he said, walking slowly off the field.

"I wanted to. You're still my best friend, remember?"

He continued to walk across the broad field, heading toward the school.

"Mind if I walk with you?" I asked, running to keep up with him.

"Guess not."

"Actually, I thought you'd want to know. . . . The institute turned me down for the summer."

"I'm sorry to hear that," he said stiffly.

"They were looking for people with scuba experience. You were right about that."

Derek didn't respond, continuing across the field in slow, measured steps.

"That was a great game you pitched," I said, matching him stride for stride.

"Thanks," he said without much emotion. "It wasn't great, though. Good, but not great."

"That's a matter of opinion." We were headed across the football field now, which without its painted white lines was nothing more than a big field of overgrown grass. "How are you doing, Derek?" I said after a while.

"Fine."

"Keeping busy?"

"Yeah. I hear you are, too. How's Sam?" he asked, the bitterness in his voice unmistakable.

"Your hearing's not so good. Sam and I have nothing to do with each other," I said, hoping to elicit a response from Derek on that one. But he kept walking silently. "You're still mad at me, aren't you?" I asked as we approached the entrance to the boys' locker room.

"I'm not mad at you."

"Good, I was worried about that."

For the first time since the conversation started, Derek turned to look in my direction. "Why?"

"Why?" I repeated. "Because I care about you very much. I want you to go on with your life without feeling I've inflicted a terrible hurt on you."

"Friends aren't supposed to hurt each other. Are you feeling guilty or something?"

"No. But I wanted to show you this." I stuck my right hand in front of his face.

"Nice hand. So?" The bitterness was still in his voice.

"What do you see on my finger?"

"The ring?" It was the one he'd given me for Christmas. "I'd figured you'd thrown that out by now."

"Don't you remember what you said when you gave it to me? You said, 'This is for the friendship we have that will last as long as there are waves in the ocean and fish in the sea.' "

He looked surprised. "I said that? Sounds pretty corny to me."

"Maybe. But I accepted this ring under those terms, and I'm not about to throw it away now."

That seemed to soften him a little, and I thought I detected the beginnings of a smile on his face.

"I've got something to say to you—as a friend," I went on. "You're doing no one any good moping around for me. Especially yourself. There was another girl in the stands watching you today who likes you a lot. I'm not saying you have to like her or even fall in love with her or anything like that. But give some thought to rejoining the dating world. You know the prom is coming up in another month, and the scramble for dates is going on. If you want to go, you'd better act now while the selection is still good."

We'd come to the back door to the boys' locker

room, and Derek turned to face me. "Thanks for the pep talk. I'll think about it," he said. But from the lack of expression in his voice, I couldn't tell if any of what I'd said had gotten through.

Wondering if I'd only made matters worse, I walked dejectedly toward home.

Chapter Eighteen

The house was quiet when I got home. Natalie was nowhere in sight. She'd been coming home later and later recently, and I think it had something to do with a boy named Doug. I was glad at least one of the Mallory girls had spring fever.

By now I'd talked myself into believing my conversation with Derek had been a waste of time. Not once had he made an effort to seem the least bit interested in me or what I had to say. He seemed so bitter I doubted he'd ever want to speak to me again, let alone want to be friends. That thought sank me into about as low a depression as I'd ever been in.

I got out the mixing bowl and made a batch of brownies. I put the batter in the oven and sat at the table thinking that even brownies wouldn't be enough to cheer me up this time.

I'll just keep eating these things till I blow up like a small balloon and nobody will want to have anything to do with me, I told myself, trying to imagine what I'd look like with a forty-six–inch waistline.

Chuckling over that funny image, I opened the back door to let in some fresh air. Pretty soon it'd be time to run the air conditioners, I thought, and time to look for a summer job and plan ahead for college. My life is rushing by me, I reflected with a shock, and here I am wasting part of it on being depressed. Well, I'd have to get over it. From now on, I vowed, Drea Mallory would not let life's setbacks get the better of her.

At the sound of the oven buzzer, I opened the oven door and reached in to remove the brownies. I nearly burned my hand, however, when I was startled by the slamming of the back door.

"Natalie!" I practically screamed. "The least you could do when you walk in—" My mouth hung open when I saw who it was. "Derek!"

"I smelled the brownies. Do you think you can spare a few extra ones for a friend?"

"Oh, Derek," I said, smiling. "Come on in."

"I am in."

"So you are." I laughed nervously and set the brownie pan on the oven range. "Have a seat."

"I can't stay long," he said, beginning to smile. "But I had to let you know—I don't hate you."

"You don't?"

"For a while there, I was really angry with you. But I've been doing a lot of thinking lately, and I think all those things you've been trying to tell me make sense, after all." He reached out a hand. "Friends?"

I grabbed his hand and shook it firmly. "Friends," I echoed. "Friends forever." Impulsively I grabbed his waist and gave him a bear hug, which he responded to by putting his arms around my back and squeezing me tight.

A moment of awkward silence came over us when we drew apart. OK, now what? I thought, sensing that Derek had something else on his mind.

"Drea," he began slowly. "Who's the girl you say is interested in me?"

I smiled slyly. "Why you little sneak, coming in here with your heart in your hand, sweet-talking me with this friends stuff. All you want to know about is some dumb girl!"

"That's not true!" he cried, his face reddening a little.

"Yeah, tell me about it." I tried to pout in mock anger but ended up laughing heartily. "Welcome back, Derek," I said at last.

Derek walked over to where I was standing, near the refrigerator, and put his hands on my shoulders. "I'll make you a deal. If you tell me all about this girl, I'll tell you what one Clark Whitfield had to say about one Andrea Mallory."

"Clark? What'd he say?" I asked eagerly.

"Interested, huh?" Derek teased. "I always had

a suspicion that blonds were more to your liking."

"So tell me what he said."

"Huh-uh," he said, cutting into the hot brownies. "You first."

"OK. The girl is Melissa, and she was at the game today because she likes you and would love to go out with you."

"Really? She really said that?" Derek's eyes lit up, and a strange but wonderful feeling came over me as I realized I'd just played matchmaker.

I nodded and handed him a glass of milk. "Now it's your turn."

To make me squirm a little, Derek drank the entire glass before speaking. "I talked to Clark in PE, and he wanted to know what was going on with us. When I told him we were just friends now, he told me that that was good since he was thinking of asking you out."

"Really?" I squealed, then straightened up quickly. Knowing how sensitive Derek still may have been over our breakup, I didn't want to seem overenthusiastic. "Sorry, Derek. I mean, it's not every day that one of the most popular boys in school says he's interested in you."

"That's OK. I wouldn't have told you if I thought I couldn't handle it."

"Wait a second," I said. "You said you told Clark we were friends. Then why were you so cold to me out at the field?"

"So I could come back here and make up to you and eat all your delicious brownies."

"You are a strange one, Derek," I said, popping another brownie into his mouth.

"Oh—um—Drea," Derek said, still chewing. "Promise me one thing, will you?"

"Anything, Derek."

"No double dates."

"Deal," I said, reaching over to hug my best friend. At that moment I truly felt I was the luckiest girl in the world.